The Bratva's Kidnapped Bride

Forced Marriage Mafia Romance

Levov Bratva Book 1

Deva Blake

CONTENTS

Chapter 1 - Adrienne

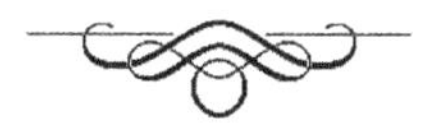

"You'll be dead in two minutes."

The man whose time of death I'd just pronounced unburied his face from a stripper's cleavage and looked at me with eyes that screamed he thought I was either a nuisance or completely crazy. All of them looked at me that way, and they ended up dying without having to regret not taking me seriously…or maybe they regretted it in the second after the bullet hit their head, before their lives drained from them.

"Who the fuck are you, bitch?" he asked, his Russian accent thick. I could see the utter disgust in his eyes as the disco lights took turns flashing green, red, and blue on him.

"Me?" I gave him a smile because I thought it was only fair for a soon-to-be corpse to be surrounded by cheerful faces in his last moments. "Adrienne, but some call me *Portatore di morte*." *Bringer of death.*

His dark eyes widened at me; their eyes always widened at me when the realization hit them. "*Morte*?"

"Some call me that too," I inclined. I turned my wrist and stared at my black watch before returning my gaze to him. "You'll be dead in thirty seconds."

He pushed the stripper away from himself, causing her to crash into another clubber who had no idea their night was about to be ruined. "*Devka*!" he roared at the top of his voice as he flew to his feet at the speed of light. He was about to retrieve something from his pocket when a loud bang silenced the room and warm liquid splattered all over my face, then the thud of a body falling to the ground followed.

The club grew chaotic with screams and the stomping of desperate feet as they tried to flee what would have become a crime scene in a normal circumstance. But this was not a normal circumstance; it was a crime family war circumstance and the body on the floor would be nowhere to be found ten minutes from now.

I lowered my gaze to him, his dark eyes wide open as blood trickled from the bullet hole in his forehead. "Rest in peace." I did not add a name because I never cared to know their names, all I needed was a picture of their faces. It somehow made the burden of taking so many lives—or at least, delivering the news of one's death to them—easier.

And to be honest, none of the people I'd delivered their deaths to since I was fourteen were innocent. Most of them were traffickers, drug dealers, rapists, and murderers. They all deserved it in one way or another.

I wasn't much different from them either.

I had as much blood on my hands as anyone else associated with the mafia.

This is the world I was born into, a world where the shedding of human blood was no different from slaughtering animals during Thanksgiving. A world where I was nothing but the bringer of death, seducer of men, and someday, a bargaining prospect for my papa, Dante Paolo. He was the bloodthirsty leader of the Italian crime family in New York, and I was his daughter in every way that mattered. *His only daughter.*

I took a bottle of whiskey off the round table beside this man's lifeless body, poured myself a shot, and said a silent prayer for his soul. *For my soul.*

Another bang came from outside. I took my time to gulp my shot and enjoy the burning sensation it created as it trailed down my throat.

"Adrienne!" I heard Ricco, my father's right-hand man, call out to me from a distance. There was urgency in his voice, and with the repeated screams and sound of gunshots outside, I presumed things were about to get messy. But then again, things were always messy in my world.

I poured myself another shot of whiskey and did a sign of the cross with one hand as I closed the man's eyes with another hand before turning to the exit.

My eyes met with murderous piercing blue eyes that instantly froze my limbs, practically rendering me unable to move. I gasped. Andrei Levov was standing only twelve steps away from me, wearing a dark scowl on his face with both hands hidden away in the pocket of his suit, which I couldn't quite make out the color of under the dim lighting of the now almost empty club room.

His height was intimidating from afar and I was certain he would tower over me if we stood close to each other. My eyes strayed to his chest for a second, and then to his shoulders. He was so well-built and muscular that it made me wonder if he was really forty-two.

And his face, there was no way I could forget it, the face of my family's sworn enemy.

I hadn't met him before, but my papa had several of his pictures in his office and he had appeared on the news several times for his famous whiskey brand—the one I drank three minutes ago being one of them. He was also famous for having the largest clubs in New York.

In other words, he was famously known as one of the richest businessmen in New York.

A laugh almost escaped my lips because only those of us born in this world knew Andrei Levov for who he really was; dark, evil, vile, and a bloodsucker. Not very different from my father, *and I.*

I'd known this was one of his clubs when I agreed to lead the job tonight—not that I had much choice anyway. Dancing in volcano lava was a better option than saying no to my papa, I'd learned that before I even learned how to walk. My papa's brutal ego aside, I'd come here because I wanted to know if this Russian piece of shit was really as unkillable as they made him seem.

His eyes were still on me, scrutinizing me from a distance, as if he knew who I was and was being cautious. His gaze moved from my face to my breasts, then to every other part of my body. There was something fiery about his gaze that burned every part of me it landed on. I really felt like the better option would be to fuck him. Dammit! My attraction to older men was messing with my senses. I couldn't risk it.

I pulled out my .45 from where it was strapped between my thighs, intentionally being sensual with the hope of distracting Andrei while keeping my gaze steady on him. He was one sneaky bastard; who knew what he'd do if I dared look away.

A wicked smirk found its way to my lips as I pulled the deadly metal from my thighs and raised it till it was pointed at Andrei. One of his guys came in just then; he removed his own gun and pointed it in my direction but dropped it back down when Andrei raised a dismissive hand.

Was he daring me? Was he thinking I wouldn't have the balls to shoot him? What the fuck was he thinking? I cocked my gun to warn him, but that only had a negative effect as he started towards me.

My hand started quivering, my gun suddenly felt too heavy to carry. Cold blood rushed to my brain, and I could hear the drumming of my pulse in my ears with every step he took as he closed the distance between us.

This isn't good. Why wasn't I pulling the trigger? His presence was intimidating, his dark aura possessing everything around him, including me.

My legs itched to pace backward as he neared me, but I forced myself not to move an inch away. There was no way I'd let him see the effect he had on me. Fuck, I hated how the presence of this ruthless crime lord was affecting me. My father would spit curses to the devil if he had any idea how much of a failure I was right now.

I hadn't finished handling the turmoil in my head when my gun came in contact with a certain hardness. The only thing between me and Andrei right now was my stretched arm and the .45 it was holding.

Andrei's jaw twitched. His eyes had flames in them, and I could see the veins in his neck swell. "What is it, *malysh*?" His voice was terribly thick with a Russian accent to spice it up—just like the man whose blood splattered on me minutes ago—only, the man's voice had no spice that made my blood rush.

What the hell was I thinking? I was standing in front of the most notorious mafia boss in New York, yet I was thinking of spice and deep-voice-effects. *Get a hold of yourself, Adrienne.* "I'll shoot you if you fucking move one more time." I meant it, and although I'd rather never have blood directly on my hands, it was better to kill than to be killed.

And knowing the men in our gruesome world, death would be mercy after being kidnapped, drugged, and fucked without your consent several times. And from everything I'd heard, a man like Andrei Levov could do a lot more than that.

He opened his mouth as if to say something but was interrupted when someone shot in our direction, missing bursting his brains by only an inch. We both ducked. I looked in the direction of the shooter and saw it was Ricco.

Andrei attempted to take something out from his suit vest. I kicked his hand and tried to make a run for it but strong warm hands gripped my legs. Panic set in, I tried to kick him with my other leg, but he gripped it too, dragging me to himself with such speed that my .45 fell out of my hand.

Ricco and the other guys stopped shooting when they saw I'd been captured. Andrei's hand wrapped me steadily to himself. This wasn't the moment, but the warmness of his body was ridding me of my senses. His earthy scent filled my nose; my brain started to dissect the ingredients his perfume was made of. *Sandalwood, patchouli, and rosewood.*

"Let the girl go," Ricco's grumpy voice demanded. He was a large, tall guy with a fittingly large muscular belly and curly raven hair.

"*Pochemu ya dolzhen?*" *Why should I?* Andrei asked. His voice possessed a calmness that sent chills down my spine. "You're the ones who crossed my territory."

"Take me, let the girl go."

"No!" I shook my head at Ricco. "Don't—"

"You are mine now, *malysh*," Andrei growled. "You do not speak unless I ask you to." His grip tightened on my neck. "Drop your weapon," he said to Ricco.

I shook my head again, notifying Ricco not to drop his weapon. He looked hesitant for a while before stretching his gun out on the floor.

"Good. Now, who do you work for, *malysh*? Paolo?"

"I haven't heard of that name before," I lied. My father had once said it was best to be discrete in an attack like this. In his own words, it didn't matter if I was dying, as long as it was not an open war between the two mafia families in New York. I'd rather die in the attack than betray him. There was no mercy for anyone who did that, even if that person was his daughter.

"Do understand, child. I cannot let both of you walk out here alive."

Nothing in the world could have prepared me for what happened next. There was no warning, no bang. But there was a thud, and there was blood, spreading on Ricco's chest, and life faded away from his face.

I'd always thought Ricco was immortal, just like my father and the devil who had his arms wrapped firmly around my neck. I wanted to scream, shout, but it felt as if watching Ricco's blood paint the ground seeped away every ounce of energy I had left.

"Keep this in mind, *malysh*," Andrei said in a rough tone. "The next time I see you will be the day you die."

I nodded, holding back tears that were meant for Ricco, and making my own promise to Andrei.

The next time I see you will be the day you die.

Chapter 2 - Andrei

I have no issue killing women for one reason: my enemies have no gender.

But then, no woman had ever had the balls to point a damn gun at me. This tiny woman standing in front of me with her ass pressing against my dick was the first one.

And she'd not just pointed a gun at me. She'd dared to try and kick me in the balls. *Fucking bitch.*

The thought that I almost got kicked in the balls by a woman sent adrenaline through my veins and I tightened my arms around her small neck, threatening to squeeze the life out of her if she so much as moved the wrong way.

Strawberry and lavender scents from her white, long hair dominated the smell of alcohol, death, and pungent nitroglycerin swirling in the air. I sniffed her hair, wrapping the length of it twice in my hands as I drew her head back, making it as painful as possible.

She stiffened under my touch, probably trying her best to hide the fear that was making her legs tremble. I wondered if she was cursing me or swearing to kill me. It wouldn't be odd for a woman like her to think she had a chance at killing a man like me even though the chances of me fucking her life out of her were greater than whatever chance she had at taking mine.

"Go, *malysh*," I whispered hoarsely into her ear. "Tell him I am coming."

She took two calculated steps away from me, as if she really didn't believe I was letting her go, and she was right to think so. I was not just letting her go, I never let anyone just go, not without a souvenir to remember me by at least.

"Stop!"

She stilled in front of Ricco; I'd recognized him as Dante's most reliable man from the moment he came to save her.

And of course, only Dante would be audacious enough to try and kill my men. I knew it was a message for me to give up my control in New York to him; he'd been on my tail since I became the boss of the Bratva at eighteen. Although he was only ten years older than I was, he felt I was too young to rule New York. It was either I joined alliances and served him, or I gave up power to him.

No Levov in the Bratva family had ever given up power to a Paolo, and I wasn't going to be the first.

My uncle, *devil rest his soul*, had other ideas as he felt he deserved the throne more than I did. He'd given into his greed and joined alliances with Dante to bring me down in exchange for wielding his influence on the damned Italian mafia boss. It was atrocious that a member of the Bratva was willing to take the Russian mafia throne from his family only to hand it to an Italian.

In the end, I had no choice but to tear him apart limb by limb, sending the parts of his mutilated corpse as a warning to everyone who dared to stand in my way.

Dante Paolo was one of the men who received a special human limb package. He'd behaved himself for a few years after, but recently, he was starting to get on my nerves. I needed to get rid of that rat quickly.

Since Ricco was here, I was positive she was also linked to Dante in some way—I'd heard he had a daughter from his dead wife, but news quickly spread weeks later that the baby had died along with her mother, and this woman looked nothing like Dante so the chances of them being related were minute.

While Dante was a giant-built, slim fucker with hair as dark as his eyes and soul, this woman was average height with white hair, gray eyes, and curves that proved she wasn't one of the women who took dieting very seriously and—dammit! Those curves.

The way her black slit dress clung to them was enough to make me lose my focus. I could barely count how many times I'd imagined flipping her over the bar counter, sliding up her dress, and fucking the shit out of her.

But one of my men was lying dead on the floor and I needed to take care of him before the cops arrived. I also couldn't risk satisfying my cock with a woman who was probably thinking of all the ways she could slice my throat. *Damn!* I had to admit it though, sex with her would be a welcome change from all the spineless women I'd been fucking.

I pulled a knife from my jacket and walked to Ricco's body, lowered myself to the ground, and placed the knife on his right index finger; it was my signature to cut the body parts of my enemies, but it was no fun doing it now that he was dead. I preferred to torture my prey while they were still alive.

"Here," I said, raising the knife to the white-haired woman. "Cut it off."

A low gasp escaped her throat as her eyes widened in terror. She looked too innocent for a woman who was drinking beside a dead guy only minutes ago. Where the hell was the sassy girl who'd pointed a gun at my chest only minutes ago?

"I can't." Her protest came out very weakly.

"*Malysh*." I raised myself to my feet and edged towards her till I was towering above her. "I wasn't giving you a choice."

"Neither was I asking you for one." She growled her disagreement this time, like a large feline scaring off its prey. Only she was the prey now, and I was the predator. She closed her eyes, cleared her throat, and then gave me a stern glance. "I won't."

I let my lips form a crooked smile. Having a woman turn down my command was something I'd just experienced for the first time since I was old enough to give commands. This woman was crossing every line with me. I should've been upset, but I found her amusing instead. I wanted to test the waters and discover how much she'd let me get away with until she fully snapped. "Either you cut it off…or I punish you."

"Punish me." Her gaze worked its way from my chest to my neck, and then slowly to my face till our eyes met. Dried blood smeared the skin on half of her face, and her eyes took several colors in the changing lights.

If only she had an idea of the many ways I could punish her. I would have those ways for next time, though; I had a feeling we'd be meeting again soon. "Very well then." I walked behind her and wrapped her hair in my hand, twice, so that only the length reaching her shoulders was free from my grasp. In one quick slash of my knife, her waist-length hair fell short, only reaching her shoulder. Her white hair looked better that way, fitting for a sassy woman.

I lowered myself to her ears. "Dante Paolo, tell him I will have his head soon," I whispered dryly.

She spun very quickly to me. I could see her eyes dilate with dread. Her chest was rising too quickly, as if a volcano was erupting inside. "Dante Paolo had nothing to do with this."

"Does he not?" I grabbed her jaw and tilted her face toward mine. "Lie to me again and your tongue will be out of your mouth faster than his head would roll off his neck."

She threw her head from side to side trying to wrestle free from my grip on her jaw, but I didn't give her the chance to. "I've heard people say you're unkillable." She smiled softly, cruelly. "I may end up proving them wrong."

I heard the sound of a spray followed by the feeling of pepper in my eyes and footsteps as she ran away. *"Fucking—"* I growled, struggling not to rub my eyes. Another set of footsteps approached, and from the heaviness of them, I could tell it was Alexei.

"*Brat!*" Brother. I could feel his eyes scrutinize me for a moment. "I'll get her." He tried to move away but I grabbed him by the hand and pulled him back.

Tears escaped my eyes as I forced them open, trying to escape the sting from the pepper spray. I was lucky she hadn't chosen the more terrifying option, acid. "Let her go."

Alexei looked at me with eyes that demanded further explanation. Although he was forty, only two years younger than I was and taller than me by three extra inches, he'd been my right-hand man since I was eighteen and he was sixteen. He gave the best advice and once scooped out a man's eyeballs from his socket just because he glared at me the wrong way.

I had two other brothers, Dimitri and Isidor. Dimitri was three years younger than Alexei, and though he was just as gruesome and huge as

Alexei, it was not out of complete loyalty. It was safe to say he enjoyed playing the devil on Earth.

Isidor, on the other hand, was a teenage boy in the body of a thirty-five-year-old man who loved to do nothing other than party, drink, and fuck half the women in New York. I didn't care what he did with his dick in his free time, but my shit of a brother caused more problems for me than the people craving my head on a pile of ammunition.

"Leave her for now." I turned to where my man's body lay. His veins must have run out of blood because his forehead was no longer bleeding and I thought if I pointed a torch, I could see his brains. "Clean this shit up first."

My brother still had his eyes, which were the same cloudless sky blue as mine, fixed curiously on me, as if he wanted to say something but was contemplating it.

"Find out who she is."

"Adrienne Paolo," Alexei said, almost cutting me off. "Dante Paolo's daughter."

"Dante's daughter did not die?"

"No." *Dante, cunning bastard.* "He kept her hidden for years. She's seduced two of our men, lured them into a room, and had them killed. She's also delivered the time of death of four of them." He paused. "They call her *Morte.*"

I shot an angry glance at Alexei. "You kept all this hidden from me?"

He put on his most indifferent expression. "I wanted to tell you only after I'd gotten all the information about her."

"There is no time for that." I clenched my fist on Adrienne's hair in my hands. The only difference between me and Dante was one thing. I keep those close to me safe while the piece of shit used his only daughter as a weapon, the same way he used his wife to make a baby twenty-one years ago even though he knew it would kill her.

Right! How could I miss the uncanny resemblance between Adrienne and Isabella, with the same white hair and searching gray eyes? She'd not died, she'd grown to be a beautiful woman just like her mama, and she's her papa's weapon.

I'd turn that weapon into mine and end the Paolo lineage with it.

"Find her and bring her to me."

Chapter 3 - Adrienne

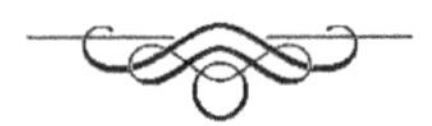

Andrei Levov was killable after all, and that was all I needed to know.

He was like every other egotistical man in the mafia world, looking down on women and feeling impenetrable. Too bad his death would also be at the hands of a woman.

That woman would be me.

I reached for my hair and felt my new haircut. I'd probably thank him before I killed him; I'd always hated my long hair because my papa had a weird obsession with it. There were times when he was drunk that he'd call me Isabella. I often wondered if that was my mother's name. If it was, did he love her? If he did love her, why did he work so hard to make sure I had nothing to remember her by?

Many questions flooded my mind, and so did Andrei's face. I could imagine how pale his piercing blue eyes would be when I drained the life out of him. How hard would his large frame thud to the ground when his consciousness ceased to exist as my bullet created a hole in his skull?

I'd sworn never to do the dirty work of getting blood on my own hands, but if it meant I'd rid New York of the rule of a horrible tyrant, I'd even have a blood bath.

Ridding New York from the vile ruling of the mafia was not limited to Andrei. My father was just as bad as him, but I couldn't drive a bullet straight into my own father's head. I'd think of what to do with him after I used his power to wipe Andrei and his organization out of existence. At least now I knew he wasn't the immortal mafia boss they made him out to be.

I'd confirmed he was just as killable as every other man.

And at the cost of Ricco's life.

Ricco had faithfully been by my papa's side for twenty-seven years, which was approximately six years before I was born, and although he was no better than my papa when it came to the thirst for blood, he'd been the most loyal dog, as my papa had always referred to him as. I'd thought my papa referred to him that way to exert his authority, but I was wrong.

I'd expected my papa to be sad after Ricco's death. I'd expected him to rage and curse down the whole Bratva family. But he didn't. He only said okay and dropped the call. Five minutes later, he sent an address and pictures to my phone which he tagged *the second job for tonight.*

The second job was a six-year-old boy and his mother, the son and the wife of the man I'd just watched die in front of me two hours ago. I heard the mother cry as she called her son's name.

"Aleksandr!" she squealed in the dark as three of my father's men dragged her from her white brick-layered bungalow that gave view to a garden of roses and hyacinths. *Aleksandr,* this was the first time I'd heard the name of anyone before telling them when they'd die.

The gentle night breeze tingled my skin and filled the air with the scent of the flowers, and I closed my eyes, imagining being from a normal world. A world where I was allowed to plant a garden and play with dolls rather than this world where all I learned was how to kill a man with one stab.

I opened my eyes as a heard silent sobs and footsteps. My papa's men threw the mother and son in front of me, ruining my peace as hyacinths and roses faded into the smell of corpses and shattered brains. It made me nauseous. *I hate this life.*

The mother crawled to her son and wrapped him protectively in her arms while he stared at me with brown eyes that sparkled under the dim moonlight. I imagined if that was what a mother's love felt like. Protective. Sacrificial. "Who are you? What do you want from us?" Her voice was shaky, and her hands vibrated as she clutched her son, glaring sharp claws at me like a mama bear, ready to tear anyone who tried to harm her baby into a million pieces. Too bad she wasn't actually a bear, and the guns pointed at her would do far more damage than a bear's claws ever could. And quicker too.

I wanted to do my usual thing; pronounce their time of death and leave the rest to my father's men, but one glance at the duo—the innocence in the boy's eyes as he probably didn't even know he was about to die, the genuine fear and sadness in the mother's eyes as tears sheeted down their face—she must've not even known her husband was dead.

Air stalled in my lungs, making it hard for me to breathe. *I hate this, I fucking hate it.* "I am sorry…" I hesitated. "Goodbye." That was all I was able to say before turning my back on them. My father's men cocked their guns.

"Please, don't do this." Her plea came out like a desperate cry. "You can kill me, just let my son go. Please, I'm begging you."

My head began to spin, and the image of all the men I'd seen die flashed before my eyes. All had been the type of men I despised, none had been a child or an innocent woman. I couldn't take it. The mere thought of seeing Aleksandr's body among them made me sick.

He didn't deserve it.

He doesn't deserve to die.

I held my stomach and swiveled to them. "Don't shoot!" Panic crept from my stomach and into my throat. "Don't fucking shoot."

Confusion covered the men's faces like a Halloween makeover. They must've thought I was crazy or something. "I'll shoot you if you fucking shoot." I couldn't hold it anymore. The disgust I'd always felt for myself, the passionate loathing I'd had for my papa since I was old enough to loathe someone, rushed to my throat, causing the muscles in my esophagus to contract as I bent over to let it all out.

The last time I puked on a job was when I watched someone die for the first time, eleven years ago. It had been on my tenth birthday. My papa had forced me to watch as he ripped out a man's throat—when I got scared and looked away, he made me sleep in a pool outside for the first time. I couldn't remember what happened next, but I woke up in the hospital three days later to his frown towering above me as he called me, "*Debole.*" Weak.

One of my father's men, Enzo, covered with muscles that were too big for his body and a beard that was long enough to be braided, still had his gun pointed at the mother and son. My senses departed me, and my body had a mind of its own. I walked to him and grabbed his gun. "Shoot at them and you're dead."

Enzo scoffed. "What the fuck are you doing, bitch?"

I raised his gun at him. "Call me a bitch one more time and that will be the last word you say."

There was reluctance in his eyes for a while. "I don't work for you, *ragazzina.* I work for your father." He stared down at the gun. "

"My words stand in my father's absence." I cocked the gun. "You think I won't kill you? Try me."

Enzo and I fixed our eyes viciously on each other for the next five minutes. He scoffed, "I am only letting this go because of your papa." He nodded to the other men, and they retreated to the car.

"Leave this city, and never come back," I said to the mother without bearing my gaze on her.

"Thank you," she muttered with a tearful voice. "Thank you."

I did not reply because there was nothing to say. I had to think of other things, like the excuse I'd give my father for going against his orders. And my hair…fuck, I wondered how he'd react to it. Seeing how much he had always been obsessed with my hair, I was certain he'd mourn it more than he'd mourn me if perchance I died while trying to kill Andrei.

Two hours later, the car pulled over in front of the old Paolo manor that looked more like a haunted castle than it looked like a mansion. It was a tall black building with ancient dark pillars and old limestone walls. It was chilly, although it was summer, and smelt like freshly cut grass and wet sand.

Despite the fact that I've lived here since I was a kid, the view of this house crawled underneath my skin like bloodworms, giving me chills, as if the ghost of all the souls we'd murdered will escape purgatory and come to hunt us at night. I rushed inside because I hated the eerie feeling I got outside.

Animalistic moans came from inside the mansion as I climbed the stairs and reached the foyer. I knew what those moans were and who they were from, I'd grown accustomed to that disgusting sound since I was old enough to know what disgusting was.

I knocked lightly on the door to notify them of my presence before twisting the silver handle and letting myself inside the equally dark interior that was barely lit by a hearth. Black men's shoes, a black three-piece suit, a red heel, and a black dress drew a map on the floor, leading me to the living room where a woman was riding my papa like her life depended on it, moaning in a way that made vomit climb up my throat again—she was the fifth woman riding my papa this week, and it was only Wednesday.

"Papa."

She stopped riding him and looked at me with eyes that glittered in the hearth-lit living room. I glanced at the light switch across the room from me. I should've turned it on, but seeing my father's cock was not something that interested me; it would just make me vomit, and I'd had enough vomiting for one night.

My papa pushed the woman away from his body and quickly reached for his robe on the floor. At least he had a bit of shame left. The same could not be said for the woman that was riding him as she held a seductive smile at me, making her large breasts bounce as she picked her clothes up from the floor. I was certain she did it intentionally.

She paused when she reached me, made her smile even broader, and gave me an I'd-like-to-fuck-you wink before departing the room.

I finally turned on the light when I was certain my papa had clothed himself.

He grabbed a bottle of liquor and poured himself a drink, then sat on the chair that had surely seen more naked women on it than a male porn star's dick.

"Come here, child," my papa said, his voice calm yet terrifying. My papa was the human representation of a slow poison. He spoke so calmly that you never knew whether he was pleased or upset.

I neared him with cautious steps and squatted in front of him. He ran his hand through my hair, and I could see a darkness in his eyes that showed he hated my new hair. But I loved it. It felt like I'd begun my journey of cutting off my papa when Andrei chopped off half my hair. To him, he was punishing me, but to me, he'd given me a gift.

Papa's dark eyes lingered on my hair for a while before he grabbed my chin, gently at first, like he always did to reward me when I obeyed his order like the good, obedient bitch he'd trained me to be. Then his grasp tightened, his rough arm digging into my skin. "*Figlia mia.*" My child. "You disobeyed me."

My chest squeezed instantly, pressing my heart together as my blood ceased to pump. "It is not like that, Papa." I hadn't thought of an excuse, I hadn't thought of anything, but then it wouldn't matter what I told him, his ego would dominate any explanation I could muster to give him.

"Of course, it isn't." There was venom edging in his tone as he spoke, as if he was cursing me somewhere in his mind for not being a son who would inherit his bloody throne after him. Sometimes when Papa looked at me like that, I too felt regret for not being a son, but other times, I was glad I wouldn't end up becoming the same monster he was. Because I was not a son, I was a daughter.

A daughter who will put an end to this bloody underworld of ours.

He removed his hand from my hair, grabbed his glass of whiskey, and stood up. "*Entra.*" Come in. The back door opened and servants rushed in with bowls and a kettle with steam pouring out of its stout. I flew to my feet, wanting to let the anger in my heart pour out as tears, but holding it back because I couldn't afford to show any weakness.

My papa had an odd satisfaction whenever he was causing pain to someone else—I couldn't give him that satisfaction, so I stiffly watched as the servants filled the bowls with water. I didn't wait for him to tell me to step inside, I'd stopped waiting for him to ask when I was twelve.

Hotness raged against my feet as they met the water. A scream stalled in my throat and tears clouded my vision. Pain, there was pain in my feet, but somehow, it was nothing compared to the one in my heart. I clenched my fists, closed my eyes, and absorbed it all.

The water started to cool after ten minutes. I stepped out as per my papa's instructions and waited for the servants to refill the bowl with another kettle of boiling water before stepping back in again.

The cycle continued for an hour before he decided I'd had enough punishment for the night. I glanced at the white clock hanging above the hearth. It was thirty minutes past eleven, almost midnight. I stepped out of the water with my feet sore and soft, as if they would peel off if I stepped on them with too much pressure, or maybe just melt like a candle. I remember that the first time he made me step into hot water, I'd cried so much and been in so much pain that I crawled up to my room afterward, and I could barely walk for weeks.

I was still in so much pain, but I'd grown tough enough that I could hide my pain inside and walk away without a single tear dropping.

"Adrienne," he called out to me when I reached the staircase. I swiveled to face him, careful not to cause further damage to my cooked feet.

Remorse was an even worse enemy that never had a place in my father's heart as only darkness gloomed in his eyes. "I signed a contract today." He sipped his liquor. "You're getting married."

The world stilled and my pulse halted as I repeated my papa's words in my head. *You're getting married.*

Chapter 4 - Adrienne

The laughter from the foyer was poison to my ears. My papa had told me he'd signed me off like I was one of his properties, but what he'd not told me was who my soon-to-be husband would be.

I glanced at the ice bucket, arranged with bottles of unopened whiskey across from where I was seated on the table of our gold and black dining room, swallowing my saliva and trying to keep myself from stretching my hand, grabbing a bottle, and gulping the whole thing down. I was curious, almost desperate to meet my—*I hate to say it*—new owner. That was the only knot in my stomach that I wish would unknot itself. Knowing my papa, I'd actually be surprised if my future groom was a marriage prospect, but the deep old voice that came from the foyer said other otherwise.

A whirlwind swept my thoughts to the only place it had no business being, Andrei. Not that I liked him or anything serious, just that he was forty-two, which was almost twice my age. Yet he looked nothing like his age with dark, gelled hair that was brushed to the back, toned muscles that were visible beneath his suit—

My God, what was I thinking about?

Spiders crept up my spine—I had arachnophobia—as the voices in the foyer drew closer and closer till they filled the room. My jaw dropped to the ground as Mario Luigi stepped into the dining with my papa. He was my papa's underboss, older than him by about six years. He has a son who was my senior by ten years. Maybe that was a good thing, maybe it was his son he wanted me to marry and not him. The chances of that were slim, but I was determined to hold onto the last thread of hope I could.

"Adrienne."

I stood to welcome our guest, *or my future husband,* as my papa called my name. I put on my most polite-yet-pretentious smile with my hands threaded together and my stomach churning with anxiety.

Mario walked over to the table, took my hand, and placed the most disgusting kiss on it. "You're just as beautiful as you've always been, my dear Adrienne." He was still holding my hand and brushing it with his thumb as if he was trying to send a signal to the rest of my body.

I am going to puke. "Welcome to our home, Mario." My facial muscles were tense. I feared my smile would break into a dragon-frown if I didn't stay conscious of it.

"This home will not be your home very soon, *cara mia."* His eyes rested on my cleavage. I was dressed in a green designer turtleneck and knit dress, nothing provocative, so I wondered why he was displaying such animalistic behavior. "Your home will be with me, in my mansion," he boasted with a smile as if he'd achieved something huge. I guessed buying a prisoner was something huge to him, just like it was to every other man in our dark underworld.

Then his sentence became clearer than it was the first minute I heard it. *"Your home will be with me, in my mansion."* I pulled my hand away from Mario and took two paces away from him. I glanced at my papa; his face was bright with a beaming smile.

"You're to marry Mario in a month, *ragazzina*," my papa said. "A date has been fixed."

I moved back several paces again until my back hit the gold drape covering the white concrete walls of the old Paolo manor. "I won't marry him." The protest was out of my mouth before I could stop it.

"Yes you will, Adrienne," my papa said firmly. "Now enough with the drama, let's eat."

"I will not marry him," I repeated. It was louder and more violent that my first protest. My eyes began to sting and blood raced to my head, making me want to scream. "I will not marry this old fuck, Papa."

Mario's eyes widened at the same time my papa's did. Women had many rules and restrictions in this suffocating organization, and the summary of those rules was: thou shall not do anything unladylike.

Ladylike by the men's standard was women simply being robots and baby-popping machines. So, I understood where their shock came from as I cursed. After all, it had probably been two centuries or more since they heard a woman speak foully.

"Did you hear me, Papa?" I asked, hearing the cracking of my voice as it rang in my ears. "Kill me, do whatever you must, but do not force me into a marriage with a man who is almost three times my age." I paused and waited for a response from my father. I wasn't sure what I was expecting but any reaction at all would be better than the grave silence in the dining room as two pairs of stunned and furious eyes glued themselves on me.

Mario must have overcome his initial shock because after what seemed like an eternity, he started towards me. "You need to be taught some manners, bitch." He raised his hands at me but ceased to carry out his intentions of slapping me when my papa called his name.

"She is not yours yet, Mario," my papa said with a tone calmer than the ocean. "I will handle my daughter myself." It felt like my papa was coming to my defense, right? Wrong. Truth is, I'd have preferred to be stroked and starved, but with his silence, I knew a hurricane was forming.

He walked out of the dining room without giving me as much as a glance. I went and sank onto one of the dining chairs, hoping Mario would not hear the way my heart was pounding in my chest as my brain rummaged through a million thoughts of what my papa would do if he returned.

The door creaked open again immediately. Enzo and a few other of my papa's men were with him. My eyes trailed to Enzo's hand; he was holding a whip that looked like it had just been borrowed from a stable.

Fear gripped me. What was he going to do with that? Was he going to whip me? My palms were sweaty, my legs were weak, and my feet became sore all over. "Papa—" Enzo and two more of my papa's men held me tight and bent me over the dining table, steadying me as my papa used the whip on my back. *One, two, three, four... fifty.* I didn't remember much of what happened afterward.

My back was throbbing with pain, my tears were threatening to fall without my permission, and whatever was left of my heart, of the love I had for the man who was supposed to be my father, vanished.

I bit back every pain I was feeling and glared at my father through misty eyes, but only met darkness, hatred, and anger. There was no remorse. My papa liked to think his biggest enemy was Andrei, but it wasn't. It was remorse that was his truest rival.

And then I glanced at Mario. His eyes had perverted amusement and his teeth flashed yellow as he laughed. His wild laughter rang in my ears even as I turned away and limped up the stairs leading to my bedroom, until I entered my room and shut the door behind me.

Darkness almost clouded my room, save for the slash of moonlight that shone through my window like a silver sword. I didn't want moonlight or any light at all; it was best to remain in the dark, thinking what I'd been thinking for twenty-one years, feeling the same I'd felt on days like this for twenty-one years. Panicking. *I need to escape.*

Sweat suddenly started dripping down my forehead, chills crept up my spine and my heart started to drum, pounding as if it needed the nearest exit from my chest, the same way I needed to exit this world—this house. *I need to escape.* I clutched my throat as my room suddenly felt too tight, leaving me breathless. *I need to escape,* that was all I could think. My panic attacks were always bad, but why the hell was I knotting my bed cover around my window?

Why the hell was I climbing down from my room?

Where was I going?

I kept walking down the dark deserted road, barefooted, with pain shooting all over my back, breathless, and with tears clouding my sight. *Fuck.*

I reached the busy roads, and then I saw the glittering pink and blue signboard that said, "Levov Night Club."

Why the fuck was I here? Why did I keep walking till I entered the crowd that smelt like sweat and alcohol?

Blue.

Blue eyes stared at me from the crowd.

Those blue eyes belonged to my enemy, *Andrei Levov.*

CHAPTER 5 - ANDREI

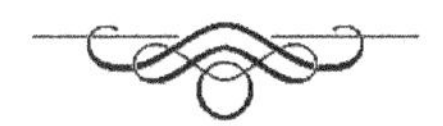

The first thing I noticed was the way the tips of her hair made contact with her shoulder. Most men liked women with long hair, but I liked mine to be distinct—short hair with smoky eyes was my kink. And that was exactly how she looked when she walked into my club, fearlessly.

Adrienne Paolo didn't strike me as a woman who would be stupid enough to walk into a den of vipers, so there could be only two reasons she would do so.

One: this was a fucking trap, probably set up by Dante Paolo.

Two: she was actually stupid.

I preferred to go with the first option because the second wasn't only very unlikely, but it was safer never to underestimate your enemies. And as it seemed, I had more enemies than friends.

Our gazes were locked on each other, hers cautious, mine observing. Her gray eyes glittered something sad in the disco lights, her lashes were wet, her black mascara smeared beneath her eyes. She looked nothing like she did when I first met her a week ago. I supposed this is what it meant when people said someone was a ghost of themselves.

I let my eyes trail briefly to her feet, and that was when I noticed she was barefooted. Dimitri had a gun to her forehead before I could take my eyes away from her *bare feet.* He looked at me and I nodded at him, my signal for him to take her inside my office. He lowered his gun behind her waist. I wasn't the type of guy to give a fuck about what body part of a woman was touched but I kept my cool and followed them as they walked to my office at the V.I.P. section.

Dim warm white light replaced the previous blue, red, and green as the three of us entered the office. Dimitri and Adrienne halted in front of my mahogany desk, and I walked past them and sat on my black-leather swivel chair before scrutinizing Adrienne some more. I thought to add one more option to the other two I'd stated. *Three: she needs something from me.*

Although that was very likely the reason why she came here looking so tattered and homeless, I still had to take necessary precautions. A Paolo was never to be trusted, especially not one who seduced men to their deaths.

"Strip," I said simply.

Adrienne raised her head quickly. "What?"

I rested back on my swivel chair and repeated myself. "Strip." *Because I need to make certain you aren't here with a weapon.* I didn't bother to add my reason though.

Adrienne glared at me for a good minute or two. She must've coded what I meant because she turned to Dimitri. "Do you think I'd be comfortable taking off my clothes in a room alone with two men?"

"I see no reason why you shouldn't." She returned her eyes to me. "You were comfortable stripping in front of more than one man when you had my men killed."

She exhaled exhaustingly. "Fine." She tried to bend but paused and bit her lips tight as if to hold back a pain of sort. I wondered if something was wrong.

I eyed Dimitri to leave. He eyed me back to say he didn't want to. The son of a gun really did know how to get on my nerves sometimes. "Get the fuck out of here," I growled at him. He spared Adrienne a suspicious glance before walking away.

Saying I wanted him to leave because Adrienne was uncomfortable with his presence was a better excuse, but I didn't want him to see her naked for some reason, and I would have asked him to leave regardless of if she wanted him to or not.

Adrienne pulled her green knit dress down to her waist and then slid it off her feet, leaving only her black net pant and bare teardrop breasts that bounced as she moved. The nipples on them were pink and it was hectic for me not to imagine myself groping them and twirling my tongue on them teasingly.

My brain fizzled and blood rushed to my groin. *Fuck,* I was having a hard-on just looking at her.

"You should be a gentleman and not stare at me as if you want to devour me," she said firmly with a brow raised at me. "It is not very polite," she added.

A perverted smirk touched my lips. "I am not a gentleman, *malysh.*" Seeing as she was Dante's daughter, she probably knew the type of reputation I had. I found it insulting she'd think I could possibly be a gentleman. "Do not ever assume that I am."

She nodded sardonically. "As much as I want to continue the argument on you being a gentleman, I am here for a different reason." She looked at a black club cushion across from her. "May I take a seat?"

For someone raised by a pig like Dante Paolo, I had to admit she was as polite as she was deadly. "You may." I made eye contact with the side of her back as she walked to the cushion. There were swollen red marks on it indicating someone had hurt her. Someone had manhandled my *malysh.*

It was odd to me how my horny state was swiftly replaced with the gritting of my teeth and clenching of my jaw. Who the fuck had dared to touch what I'd claimed as mine? "What happened to your back?"

She paused when she reached the couch and spun to face me. "It's nothing." She sat down and stared at the walls that were the color of her eyes. I knew she was lying by the way she avoided my gaze.

"Do not lie to me, *malysh.*" My voice was harsh with rage and thirst for blood. I stood from my swivel chair, went to her, and dragged her up from the cushion before examining her back. Red and purple lines crossed each other countless times, and the skin around them was crimson, darker than red.

I ran my finger on them, causing goosebumps to appear on her skin. "Who did this to you, *malysh*?" I asked again, hearing the roar in my voice.

Adrienne swallowed. "It's nothing." It was something, and it all made sense. Her entering my territory even after I'd threatened to kill her the next time we meet, her bare feet, her pale face, and misty eyes.

"Listen, *malysh*." I tilted her chin up and peered straight into her gray eyes. "The day I find out who did this to you will be the last day they breathe." It was a promise I fucking meant, and I'd fulfill that promise soon enough. That I was sure of.

She grinned, not too brightly but not too darkly either. "What does it concern you that I'm hurt? You promised to kill me, remember?"

Her breasts were way too close to my chest, and like unlike poles, I was being magnetized to her. "I'll break you, and then I'll kill you." I brushed my thumb on her lower lip. It was a pink, soft, full lip. "Till then, *malysh*, only I have the right to—" I leaned down to her ear. "To touch you," I whispered.

I heard her breath cease as a low grunt escaped her throat. It was the reaction I wanted, but then she pulled away from me. "I am not yours or anybody's, I came here for one thing, and you must help me."

I put on my most indifferent look and took a seat on my desk. "Your papa is an enemy of the Bratva family, which I rule. Why would you come to me for help?"

"Because you're the only one who can defeat the man I want to bring down." She sat down on the edge of the cushion. "My papa does not stand a chance; he and that man are too identical."

Was she trying to play a game with me? Her papa was the only person in New York that could challenge me, although I could easily take him down if he weren't busy hiding like a rat. "Say I could help you destroy whomever it is you want me to help you destroy. Why would I want to do that?"

"Because we have a common goal," she replied firmly. "The bigger picture may be blurred, and you can't really see it now, but you'll eventually come to see I'm on your side."

Laughter itched the back of my throat and I let it out. "You're on my side? *Malysh*, you pointed a gun at me a week ago! And more of my men have died because of you than have died in an open fight between the Italians and the Russians."

"I know."

"If you do, then tell me what the hell you need my help for, and I might just consider it." She really was Dante's daughter, tricky, doing her best to outsmart me, but I'd been in this game for years before she was born.

She heaved a heavy sigh. "I can't tell you unless you promise to help me out."

"I don't make blind promises, *malysh.*" That was an unspoken rule in this dark underworld and rules aside, my promises didn't hold water, so I didn't bother giving them out.

"I'll give you something else in return," she blurted desperately.

I held back a chuckle. I didn't see anything she had to offer, except her body. *Dammit!* I hated those marks that distorted her satin olive skin. Finding out who the hell hurt her was a good exchange for helping her deal with whatever the fuck she needed me to deal with, unless, of course, she wanted me to give up my life, then that would be a capital *NO*. "Tell me who hurt you, and—"

"I'll give you Dante Paolo in return."

My eyes pinned on her in one swift glance. Was she joking or trying to bait me? Her face was stern, the rage in her eyes sincere. I could see past the way her fists were clenched by her side; I'd gotten my answer on who dared to hurt her.

I'd give him a fate worse than death, and for every stroke on her back, he'd get double in return. But I had to make her mine first.

"You want to give me your father in return?"

She nodded. "Yes."

I scoffed. "Do you think I would believe that you would give your father up?" Adrienne was a child, maybe not in her looks but in how she thought I would fall so easily for her silly lies.

"You should," she answered boldly. "I am the only one who can deliver him to you, and I always keep to my words."

The Italians are proud bastards, they cut each other's throats and drink each other's blood, but one thing they never do is let others infiltrate them. And my sweet little Adrienne is one of them.

My lips curled into a wicked smile. "Prove it, and I will help you."

Her eyes burned with determination, and I could read through the stern expression on her face. "I will do whatever you want."

"Even if I ask for your blood?"

"I don't care, I've lost too much blood to care how much more I will lose."

Adrienne was bold, too bold for her own good.

I stood up and went to a small fridge in the corner of my office. "You seemed to enjoy my liquor last time." I pulled out a half bottle of liquor and two shot glasses from the fridge and brought them to her.

She looked at the shot glass I propelled to her and then at my face. "I don't want to drink."

"I wasn't asking if you want to." I shoved one of the shot glasses into her hand and filled it with brown liquor before pouring one for myself. "You're in the business, you should know sharing liquor is a way of sealing a deal."

She took the shot glass to her nose and inhaled it before cautiously taking it to her lips. She pinched her face into a grimace when the hot and bitter liquid passed her tongue and her throat moved as she swallowed it.

"Does this mean we have a deal?" she asked, bringing the shot glass away from her face. "Will you help me now?"

I smirked at her then turned around and returned to my seat. "There is one more condition before our deal is sealed."

"Don't play games with me, Andrei."

"I'm not, but I can never be too careful with an Italian, a Paolo at that."

Her hands trembled with anger and her eyes were spitting venom filled with rage at me. "Tell me, what is this condition?"

"Good girl." I gulped my liquor in one drink and set the empty shot glass on the table. "You must marry me, *malysh*."

Chapter 6 - Adrienne

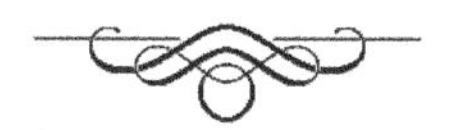

Tonight, I made a deal with the devil against my will, and I had a feeling it would cost me my life.

When I walked into the Levov club an hour ago, I had no idea what the heck I was doing or why I was even there. But after I met Andrei, an idea flashed through my brain. Killing two birds with one stone, that's exactly what I was going to do.

I was between two devils I needed to destroy: my papa and Andrei. Andrei was notorious and ruthless, so I'd heard, but he appeared a saint compared to my papa. For instance, my papa would have shot me on sight if I'd launched an attack on his club, but Andrei didn't.

On one hand, Andrei seemed to care that I was hurt, on the other hand, my papa was the one that hurt me. I was between two evils, and now I had to choose the lesser one, Andrei. I'd use him to bring my papa down since I'd rather not have his blood in my hands. Then I'd kill Andrei and burn this fucking underworld to the ground—it didn't matter if I burned along with it.

The problem was, Andrei wanted me to marry him, and I would rot six feet under before I dared to marry someone like him. "You're crazy."

His lips curled into a crooked smile, one that was so wicked even the devil would be shivering in hell just looking at it. "I know. I wouldn't be offering to marry a murderous Paolo heiress if I wasn't."

"Dream on, pig, but I won't roll in the mud with you."

He brushed his hands over his dark gelled hair, his gaze burned firmly on my face then lowered to my bare breast, burning awareness into my skin. I pretended not to feel the impact of his scrutinizing gaze. I'd only end up distracted which I couldn't afford to be.

"You should rest up tonight. I don't want you fainting at our wedding tomorrow."

God, I want to drive a knife through this man's chest right now! "Didn't you hear me the first time?" I fired at him. "A marriage between the both of us will never happen. My answer is NO."

"No one says no to me, *malysh*."

I sneered at him. "I am glad to be the first. I gave you my word. I will deliver Dante Paolo to you, and I never make promises I don't keep."

"Why don't I believe you?" he asked, squinting suspiciously at me. Truthfully, he looked so in his early thirties that it was hard to believe he was forty-two. A throb awakened between my legs as I remembered the feeling of warmth and soft hardness from his body when he stood behind me a week ago. *Fuck*. "You are a Paolo, and the Paolos never keep to their words."

He was right, I was a Paolo, and we were known for going back on our words more often than was normal in this dirty world. But although I'd left out other details—like how I was going to kill him the moment I was done using his influence to bring my father down from his throne—I was going to keep true to my words.

"I suppose it is up to you to decide if you believe me or not, but I won't be marrying you." One rule I'd learned when negotiating with a notorious mafia leader was never to appear desperate. Give the offer and wait for him to growl for the rest, just like a dog.

"You know where to find me if you agree to my offer." I got up from the cushion, picked my dress, and slid it on. "Have a good evening, Andrei Levov."

Andrei didn't say a word in reply to what I told him; he rather appeared to be in deep thought. I could feel his stare strike my back as I walked to the heavy metal door leading out of his office, a part of me wanting him to stop me from leaving and agree to my offer. The mere thought of returning to the Paolo manor riled wicked butterflies in my stomach.

Deep blue eyes stared back at me with a face very identical to Andrei's the moment I opened the door. He was shielding the door, and he was very good at it as his huge frame made it so there was no space I could squeeze away from. Not that I was the size to squeeze my way out anyway, my curvy hips would have been the first thing to get stuck. I'd heard Andrei had three brothers. The one that led me into the club with his fucking gun on my waist was one. He didn't have a facial resemblance to these two, but his eyes had the same dark shade of blue.

This one wasn't holding a gun, but with how muscled he was, I guessed he barely needed a gun to intimidate anyone. The guy looked like he would crush a skull into smashed marshmallows with very little effort, and seeing as he was unmoving from the door, he was giving me a cue to return inside.

I wheeled around to see that Andrei had a slight amusement pulling on his lips like the devil would have when he gained a dirty soul to torment. "Do you have anything else you wish to talk about?"

Andrei arched a raven brow. "There are many things to talk about, *malysh*. Let's start with you not walking out of that door."

"Do you intend to keep me hostage?" Realization slapped me on the cheeks. I'd walked into hell myself, and the chances of walking out were slim—at least, walking out alive.

"Do I have a reason to keep you hostage, huh, *malysh*?" Irritation edged in Andrei's voice as he left his desk and walked to me. His white musk and patchouli perfume invaded my nose, intoxicating me. "Don't be silly. I plan to make you my wife." His tone had mockery in it, as if he thought I was stupid.

My papa had always called me *"cretina."* I hadn't ever agreed as much on anything with him as I did at this moment. All the boldness and determination I walked into this club with suddenly started to escape my body as sweat. "What do you want from me?"

Andrei's amusement grew wider, darker. He cupped my face in his hand and lowered himself to my ears till his hell-hot breath tingled my skin. "Everything."

His voice pierced through my ears and sent a tremble to my feet. My back started to ache again, and my head was suddenly in turmoil for a way out of this situation. Andrei Levov was particularly known for testing his drugs on women and trafficking them, and I wasn't just a woman, I was the daughter of his most vicious rival. Only God knew what would happen to me if I let him take me captive.

I tried to sound as confident as I could manage. "I walked in here by my own will." The crack in my voice betrayed me. "You do not need to keep me captive or marry me to get anything from me. Agree to the offer and I'm all yours."

Silence lingered for a few minutes, threatening to stir a tornado in my chest. "Your will ceased to exist the moment you walked into my club, *malysh*," Andrei finally said, breaking the silence that caused turmoil in my stomach. "No. It no longer existed the moment I laid my eyes on you and I was going to come for you anyway. I do not need to accept your offer to get what I want, the same way I do not need your permission to take you as mine." He carried his thumb to my lips and brushed them softly, kindly, as if he had not just taken my freedom away.

There was no way out. His words sealed my fate. But I wasn't just going to stand around and obediently allow my captor to put a ring around my finger. If words would not work, then maybe my legs would. For the first time, I had to appreciate my papa's insistent combat training and drilling. "Fine," I forced a smile to conceal what I would do next. "You can have me, but I need a change of clothes."

Andrei scoffed in a way that sounded as if he was suspicious of my motive. Of course, he would be, he probably knew there was no way I'd just follow him, and that is exactly what I wanted him to think. "Playing tricks on me will only cost you your life, *malysh*. Do not forget it." He glanced above me to his brother. "Take her away."

As soon as Andrei turned his back on me I spun to his brother and gave him the slyest smile possible, which he did not respond to with any emotion. This one looked like the type of guy who did not find amusement in anything other than killing. He moved out of the way to let me pass. *Not a smart move.*

I buried my hands in his eyes and kicked his balls. He let out a grunt before I pushed him further away and put my feet into swift action, throwing one leg desperately in front of the other as I ran. My back was still sore, but my adrenaline was in control.

Loud music drummed in my ear as I climbed down the stairs from Andrei's office. I didn't know if Andrei or his brother bothered to chase me, and I didn't check because it would only slow down my pace, increasing my chances of being caught. I disappeared into the crowd of dancers, shuffling my way past them. The flickering green and purple lights made my eyes so sensitive that I narrowed them to control how much of the light was getting inside them.

The glass exit door of the club became visible when I'd almost reached the end of the crowd. I exhaled in relief, determined to reach it despite the heightening feeling of pain in my back and the sudden blurring of my environment. *Just one more step, you can do this Adrienne.* I reached the door, held the square handle, and just as I was about to push it open, strong arms slid around my waist, holding me back. My muscles tensed.

A familiar white musk and patchouli scent filled the air. "Do you think it is that easy to escape me?" His thick Russian accent roared in my ears. "Be a good little *malysh* and don't try to run."

His other hand crawled from my hips, then it moved till it reached and wrapped around my neck. I was running out of breath, but too weak to fight back. The exit door vanished into clouds, the music dimmed, and the only face that came to my mind was my face, smiling back at me.

My legs gave up the weight of my body, peace blanketed me for the very first time in years. I knew I'd met my end, and it was the most comforting thing ever.

Darkness was calling for me, and I did not try to fight it.

I opened my arms and embraced it.

Chapter 7 - Adrienne

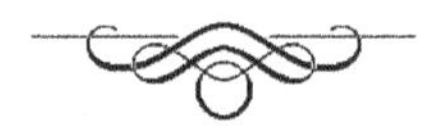

I'd never thought heaven would smell like cigarettes and alcohol, unless of course I wasn't in heaven. I was in hell.

I tried to flick my eyes open, but they felt too heavy, as if they weren't my own. I could hear voices in the background, thick masculine voices that spoke Russian. I should have taken my Russian classes more seriously than I did, but that was a regret for another day.

A wet towel dabbed my neck, and that was when one of my eyes gave in, briefly allowing me to open it for two seconds. A blurred face was close to mine, I couldn't make out the color of his eyes, but I could feel them touch my face curiously before I heard him mutter something I couldn't make out in Russian. I knew who it was as soon as I heard his voice. *Andrei.*

My eyes closed and darkness took over.

Cold soft hands were rubbing something on my back when I woke up again. I was laying on my stomach with my back facing the ceiling, cuddling the unfamiliar bed I lay on. It was cozy, warmer than the one in my room. I peeled my eyes open, taking in the view of my environment. There wasn't much in the room except an oak vanity across the bed and a standing lamp lighting the room. Drapes as red as cherries covered the windows, matching the red canopy towering above the bed and the matching red backrest.

My eyes dropped to my chest. That was when I noticed I was wearing nothing, not even panties. I tried to turn over but whomever it was that was rubbing something on my back placed her weight on me. "You should be careful; the wounds haven't healed enough."

I remained still and tilted my head up to peer at her. She had dark, raven hair that was wrapped in a bun, blue eyes like Andrei's, and a stone-cold face. She didn't look much older than I was.

"Who are you, and where am I?" I didn't know if those were the most appropriate things to say to someone who'd probably been nursing my wounds for who knows how long. And I thought asking why I was naked would be a stupid question, considering I needed to be naked for her to tend to my wounds.

"Levov estate. You passed out in the club and the boss thought it best to bring you back home," she explained. "He isn't the type to bring a woman home, so I assume you are important to him."

That sick bastard. I was important to him of course, he brought me to his home just so he could nurse me back to life and milk information about my father from me. "Where is your boss?"

She took a towel and wiped my back gently, then threw it inside a bowl of water before moving away from the bed. "You can turn now," she said, ignoring my question about where her boss was.

"Is there anything to wear?"

She tilted her head to the vanity across the bed where there were plenty of shopping bags on it from one of the biggest fashion stores in New York. "You can find something there." She lifted the bowl from the floor and started out of the room but stopped by the door.

"Boss is kind, but he is not a very patient man," she whipped her head around to look at me. "Don't try anything funny, obey him and you won't be hurt." She left the room.

I must've hurt my head really badly because I chose to misunderstand her warning. I decided I would disobey and taunt Andrei till he had no choice but to either kill me or let me go.

I stood up very cautiously, careful not to hurt my back but there was no soreness whatsoever, it was almost as if I'd not been whipped—Goddammit! How long had I been here? I'd forgotten to ask. I went to the vanity and started rummaging through the clothes there looking for something comfy to wear.

Silver dinner dress with an open back, heels, another black dress that was sleeveless and had a slit that would show off my pussy if I dared to wear it. I checked the other bags. There were more dresses that looked like they were designed for strippers, not that I minded how exposed they were, but they weren't the best options when my whole body didn't feel right for some reason.

The last bag was filled with panties and bras—I didn't wear bras, for fucks sake. A pair of tees and oversized shorts were what I needed. I slid on one of the thong panties and gave myself a butterfly hug to cover my bare breasts.

Even heaven could not have had as much white as the hallway I stepped into outside my room. Only the black ink from the still-life portraits on the walls tainted the immaculateness of it. There were no rooms close to the one I'd just come out from, but there was a staircase that I assumed led downstairs.

I descended the stairs and started to hear muffled sounds. Andrei, two brothers that I'd met at the club, and three other guys were talking by a corner close to the white doors. They didn't seem to have noticed my presence yet, but I halted on the last few stairs.

One of them glanced at me and then signaled Andrei to turn around. The moment his gaze fell on me, his brows furrowed and crimson red painted his eyes. Andrei was in a pair of blue jeans and a white tee that showed off his muscles. It pained me to admit it, but he was so freaking hot in casual clothes.

I hadn't even noticed the tattoo on one side of his arm and neck as he'd worn long sleeve button-up shirts the many times I had seen him on the news and the two times I'd met him before now. His tattoo was simple black leaves with red roses and white skulls, fitting for a man like him, alright.

He came to me and gripped me by the wrist, leading me back upstairs with such speed that I had to run to keep up with him. He dragged me inside my room and banged the door behind us. "What the heck do you think you are doing?"

"What the heck am I doing?" I couldn't tell if he was upset that I left the room or for another reason. Maybe he thought I was eavesdropping.

His eyes fell on my breasts and lingered there for a moment before trailing down the rest of my body. "You can't just walk around my house with that tiny piece of fabric around your waist and no bra."

Was he being serious? A small laugh escaped my lips. "That's considerate, considering you asked me to strip in your office not too long ago."

"You're not very smart, *malysh.*" He pulled my hands away from my breasts and shamelessly glued his eyes darkly on them as if he had the right to. I hated how my body was reacting to his gaze. "You're mine now, I'm the only one who gets to see you naked."

"I didn't give you permission to do that," I yelled. "I didn't accept to be your wife."

"I don't need your permission, *malysh*," he retorted. "I take whatever the fuck I want, including you." Yeah, he said it like a true Levov would, egoistic and possessive.

"What do we do then?" I closed the space between us. Lions mostly only attack humans when they perceive fear after intimidating them—Andrei here was no different from those proud animals, and neither was I. "What if I also want something from you?"

He held me in a chokehold, gentle enough to not squeeze the life out of me, yet strong enough to send a ball of fire running to my cheeks, making me want to melt. "All you have to do is ask me, *malysh.*" He moved so much closer that my breasts were pressed against his strong abs. I could have a fucking orgasm just being that close to him, I swear it.

"I've asked, you refused."

"Because you did not give me the answer I needed. Who hurt your back like that, *malysh*?" His dark gaze was locked on mine, gloomy, as if he would ready his gun and set out for battle if I just mentioned a name.

"I'll tell you, but I must be certain you're on my side first." *Even though I am not on your side.*

"*Horosho.*" *Fine.* He released his chokehold on my neck. "You will stay here till the day you decide to tell me who hurt you."

"I'll need some comfy clothes if I'm to stay." The words were out of my mouth before I could stop them. What the hell did I just say? Why did I even consider staying?

Andrei left the room and returned with a pile of neatly folded clothes, all black and white. "Wear these."

Are those his clothes? They smelt just like him. Was I going to wear Andrei-freaking-Levov's clothes? I was getting more excited than I needed to be—which was probably zero excitement because who gets excited just wearing their captor's clothes?

"Will these do?"

"I will manage with them for now," I replied as I unfolded them, seeing that they were all designer clothes, just the way I liked my clothes to be. Turned out Andrei and I had something in common other than the New York dark underworld we were both involved in.

Andrei leaned on the wall, watching me as I put on a pair of black baggy shorts and an oversized sleeveless shirt from the pile he brought in. "You didn't thank me, *malysh*."

Truth, I hadn't even had time to address the way he called me "*malysh*." I was not a child, especially not his, and I hated how he somehow had fun calling me that. "I suppose you know my name."

He shrugged. "I do."

"Then call me by my name."

"I won't."

I gave him a death stare, calculating how much strength I'd need to exhaust before I reached where he was standing across the room and squeezed him to death. *Fucking psychopath.* "I should call you 'daddy' since you insist on calling me a child."

His eyes sparkled mischievously as if he had a different interpretation for that word. "I like the sound of that." Sunlight spilled inside the room from outside, illuminating his white shirt and showing a not-so-clear view of the tattoo on his chest, but clear enough that I forgot how to breathe for a good second. God, this older man was gorgeous, and I wasn't even ashamed to admit it.

"You're a pervert, you know that?" I said with a frown as I sat at the vanity. "How long have I been here?" I opened the vanity to search for a brush inside.

"A week."

I raised my head at him so quickly that I feared the bones in my neck would crack. "A week?" I had been so comfortable since I woke up that I hadn't even thought of my papa; he'd be looking for me right now and only God knew what he'd do when he got to know where I really was.

A war between the two families was not what I anticipated when I left home that night. My throat became as dry as a desert and I flew to my feet. "My papa, he'll be looking for me right now." I held his gaze. "Imagine what he would do if he found out you took me against my will and married me."

Andrei narrowed his eyes at me as if I was speaking jargon. "Dante Paolo?"

"Yes," I nodded. "You have to take me back, please. He'd go to great lengths to find me and the earlier he sees me, the better."

"Better for who, *malysh*?"

Exasperation spread over me like wildfire. "You. Me. All of us." I closed my eyes, trying to hold back every punishment I'd endured. I could only imagine what he'd do to me now. "Please, take me back."

"No."

My eyes widened at the man nearing me. He halted when he was close enough to tower over me. "*Malysh*, I own you now, and if you should fear any man, that's me." He was right, even my papa had not attained the type of reputation he had, notoriously ruthless, torturous. I'd say he had been too kind to me. "You do not get the freedom to choose anything until I say so. Do you understand me?"

Evil. That is the only word I'd use to describe Andrei. But somehow, his threats were more comforting rather than terrifying. I knew physical pain and internal anguish to a fault and I doubted anyone would surpass the hurt my own father had inflicted on me, not even the king of hell himself. "Yes."

"Good. Now sit."

Like the good little girl he wanted me to be, I lowered myself onto the vanity. I was just about to ask Andrei if perchance he'd ever met my mother when a delicate feminine voice sounded in the hallway. "Andrei!"

Pure disgust took over Andrei's face as if he recognized the voice well enough to know she probably was someone he didn't want around—or maybe that is what I wished for, that it was someone he didn't want around.

"There you are." Her voice notified the room of her presence before she even entered. Vanilla and jasmine perfume followed her inside; it was the kind of scent that would knock out a person to sleep, giving them the sweetest dreams.

She was wearing designer two-piece pants and a top, a pair of red heels, and had long dark hair that reached her ass. I wish I could say I missed my long hair; I really didn't, but seeing her long raven hair made me wonder if Andrei preferred women with such hair. I sighed as I spotted my shoulder-length white hair in the vanity mirror.

"I've missed you so much," she said as she hugged Andrei, completely ignoring my existence. I didn't like her at all, and it was not because I was *jealous.* Her beauty and bright aura did not intimidate me that much, did they?

"When did you return to New York?" Andrei asked, breaking off their hug.

"An hour ago, thought I should see you first." She giggled like a teenage girl meeting her crush for the first time.

"You should have gone home to your father first."

"Why? What's wrong with paying my fiancée a visit first?"

Fiancée? My widened eyes met Andrei's before he gripped the woman's hand and dragged her out of the room, *the same way he dragged me to the room.*

It was silly of me to think that a man like Andrei—rich, handsome, and in his forties—would still be single. Even if he was, I was thick, while there were lots of slim women in the world, like his fiancée. I did not like him, but I also didn't stand a chance with him if I did.

Who am I kidding? If an option like that existed, why would he choose to be with the daughter of his rival when he could have any woman out there? It was a good thing he didn't, not like I would have chosen to be with him either. I sighed and drew my attention back to the cupboards in the vanity, failing at my attempt to erase the last minute from my memory.

The whole scenario turned to acid that burned my chest to the extent that I was feeling physical pain for no reason. Taking out a brush from one of the drawers. I started brushing my hair while thinking of the different possible ways I would kill Andrei Levov.

CHAPTER 8 - ANDREI

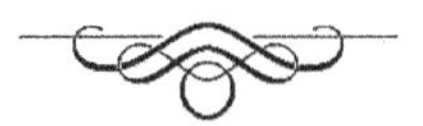

I should have anticipated how wild Adrienne Paolo would drive me before I considered holding her captive. The image of her full breasts bouncing up and down as she moved made it hard for me to think straight, and it took me thinking about bloody dead men and chopped body parts to keep myself from spanking her well-rounded ass when she turned around.

Fuck, thinking about it again was enough to make my cock hard and needy. With an ass like that, it was not a surprise how Adrienne was able to seduce some of my men to their deaths. I had a feeling I'd have ended up killing them if Dante did not beat me to it, the same way I wanted to erase the memory of everyone who was standing in the hallway when she came out of her room.

Seeing her on that staircase with a black thong and arms wrapping around her breasts made me want a personal painting of her, a painting only I could see because I'd be damned if anyone else saw my little Adrienne naked again. God help me, I might have to kill them, and I didn't give a fuck if one of them was my brother.

The sound of my name rocked me out of my dirty daze. I'd forgotten Camilla was standing right here with me. I'd dragged her out of Adrienne's room and outside to the foyer because I didn't want her infecting my sassy-little *malysh* with her nastiness, yet I'd still forgotten all about her presence because Adrienne's soft ass swaying side-to-side in those tiny panties wouldn't stop tormenting me.

I'd only met Adrienne twice, but her presence already overpowered the presence of every other woman I'd seen naked or fucked. Like this whiny brat in front of me.

"You didn't tell me your next whore would be Dante Paolo's daughter," Camilla said with her hands folded over her chest. "Tell me, does she fuck better than I do?"

Anger lingered in me. I hated Camilla referring to Adrienne as a whore, especially since Camilla was better qualified for that name. "Why? Do you have the intention of improving your skills by fucking half the men in New York?"

She rolled her eyes. "Come on, as if you also haven't fucked half the women in New York."

That was an exaggeration on her end; it was obvious she wanted me to speak of my sexcapades so she could fuel her hope once again. I wasn't going to do that. "I'm sure your number exceeds mine by far."

"Whatever," Camilla said with a wave of her hand. I hated her long artificial nails, but then again, I hated everything about her. Everything about her was fake, from her behavior to her lips, long hair, breasts, and ass. Darn! I'd never seen anyone faker than she was.

"Is there a reason why you came here unannounced?" I could barely hide my annoyance as I spoke to her.

"Why do I need to make an announcement to see my fiancée?"

One more thing I hated was how delusional she was. "I am no longer your fiancée, Camilla." I'd broken off my engagement to her six months ago after I found out she was fucking her gym instructor. I may have only agreed to marry her because of the deal I had with her dad, but cheating was something I'd never do, even to a woman as annoying as she was.

Camilla flew to Chicago shortly after with her gym instructor without showing any remorse for the shit she did. I was able to find them, and while normally I would have killed the damned instructor for touching what was mine, I'd never really considered Camilla my woman and so I didn't bother getting his dirty blood on my hands. Although, I'd made sure he never got to use his dick again, simply because he'd crossed boundaries by fucking my *fiancée.*

"Baby." She made a pouty face that disgusted me even more. "I made a mistake, and I'm sorry, alright? Can't we just make up and put the past behind us?"

Standing here with her was exasperating and the fact that she'd still never apologized but walked into my home to get me back was even more annoying. "Don't come to my home again if that is all you came to say, I don't have time for this shit."

"Baby—"

"Don't fucking call me that!" My voice was calm but edging with spiteful venom. "Shut the door on your way out." Her brown eyes watered but I didn't give a fuck, I turned my back on her and started back to Adrienne's room.

"Is this because of that fucking Paolo whore?"

Her question halted me in my track, "The next time you call her a whore will be the last time you'll have a tongue," I said without turning back to look at her.

"Isn't that a bit rude?" Adrienne's voice came from the stairs; I hadn't even noticed her standing on them. She was looking directly at me as she descended the stairs. "Calling a woman you barely know a whore, I mean, isn't it rude?"

She brushed past me and all I could think of was how well my shorts and sleeveless tee fitted her. She'd curled her hair into a bob, and I could bet all my ill-gotten money that she naturally smelt like strawberries. I swiveled to steal more glances at her as she walked to Camilla.

"Nice to meet you, I'm Adrienne Paolo." She stretched her hand out to shake Camilla's, but Camilla scoffed and slapped her hand away. Adrienne smiled psychotically and then withdrew her hands to herself.

"I know who you are," Camilla spat spitefully. "Some call you *morte,* but I think you are just a whore."

"Am I?" Adrienne's psychotic smile widened, making her look crazy as fuck. I really considered calling the psychiatric ward just in case, and maybe I was just as psychotic because I liked that crazy, killer-witch expression on her. "I think I prefer being called *morte.*"

"Well, whore." Camilla closed the space between her and Adrienne so that the fabrics of their clothes were rubbing against each other. They would have been the same height if Camilla wasn't wearing an eight-inch heel. "I have something you might want to know." She leaned in and whispered something into Adrienne's ear.

Curiosity spread all over my body. Camilla was messed up and I had no idea what shit she was saying to Adrienne, but I couldn't interfere, or maybe I didn't want to.

Camilla finished talking to Adrienne then moved back and laughed like she was demented while Adrienne still wore a firm expression, which I couldn't interpret to be shock, anger, or anything else.

"So." Camilla started to fix something invisible on Adrienne's tee. "Be a good little whore and keep Andrei entertained." Amusement beamed on her face as if she'd just won a battle.

"Didn't he say the next time you called me a whore would be the last time you had a tongue?" Adrienne didn't look at me, yet I felt as if she'd called me incompetent and unable to keep to my word. "Say that word to me just one more time, and I will rip your tongue out myself." Something about the way she said it made me feel she was really going to do it, and Camilla must have felt it too because her beam faded instantly. She gave me a brief glance before taking defeated steps out of the foyer.

Adrienne waited for Camilla to be completely out of sight before she spun around to face me. "How did you earn your reputation if you're all threats and no action?" She shook her head mockingly.

This woman had guts too big for her, and I didn't like how she challenged me one bit. Why was I letting her get away with it? "You'd be dead by now if I chose to keep to my words."

"But I'm not, which still means only one thing," Her smile twisted to one side of her face crookedly. "I'd truly kill you if I made a promise like that."

"Then why didn't you?" I asked, taking slow, steady steps to her. "Why am I not dead?" I waited for her to deny ever wanting to kill me, but she did not. Instead, she instinctively paced backward with each step I took until she hit the wall behind her.

"You're still alive because I am letting you live." Her breath was rough as I pressed my body on hers, imprisoning her between the wall and myself. "You do not have my permission to die until I get what I want from you."

Her gray eyes were blinking up at me, her cheeks were red like burning metal. I cupped her face with my hand. "Do you know why I let you live, *malysh*?"

She shook her head gently, her gaze still locked with mine.

"I'll tell you." I wrapped my hand around her waist and pulled her close till my dick was straining against her leg. I was hard and I was certain she could feel it. "I let you live because there is so much more I want to do to you before I kill you. There are so many positions I want to see you in, and you can't die until I hear you scream my name," I said, whispering into her ears as my lips brushed them.

Her breath grew ragged as if she was on fire inside, her eyes refused to peel away from me, and from her silence, it seemed I'd finally managed to leave her dumbfounded. I took my lips to hers very slowly and her eyelids fluttered shut as she probably anticipated my kiss. From the way her chest was rising and falling rapidly, I could tell she was palpitating, pumping with sexual hormones. Too bad I couldn't hear the pounding of her heart.

"What are you doing?" I asked, pulling away from her. "Did you think I'd really kiss you? Come on, I have no interest in you."

Her eyes opened and humiliation left a pink stain on her neck. I shark-smirked. "Were you hoping to get laid by me?"

"No. I was hoping to seduce you and kill you like the pig you are," she said, pushing me further away and moving from the wall, her eyes downturned with rejection or something like it.

"Too bad, *malysh*." My dick was hard, straining against my stupid jeans, and I hoped she wouldn't notice as I resorted to dismissing the strong urge to fuck her by teasing her. "You look like you were dumped in the middle of an orgasm."

"You're a dead man, Andrei Levov," she said simply and started out for the stairs, then paused and turned around, peering at my cock.

"What is it, *malysh*? Want to give me a blowjob?" I probably shouldn't talk dirty to her but right now, I was thinking with my dick, and my dick wanted Adrienne.

"For a man who has no interest in me, your cock is quite hard, Andrei Levov." She turned back to the stairs and ran upstairs.

I smiled.

Adrienne had a smart mouth, and I wanted to feel how smart she'd be when I thrust my cock inside her fucking mouth.

Chapter 9 - Adrienne

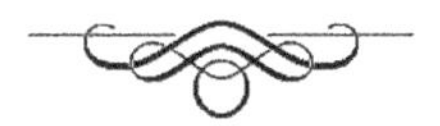

Andrei Levov really did live up to his name as a lunatic who toyed with women, and I hated how I'd manage to add myself to the list of women who became weaklings in his presence.

I exhaled, trying to blow out the frustration that had built inside of me. I closed my eyes, ashamed of myself for how easily I surrendered to his touch. Fuck. Even now, the feeling of his light touch on my face and his warm breath on my skin still lingered. Weird things were happening between my legs, tugging at my self-control and needing more of his dangerous touch.

I'd tried to deceive myself into believing my body was only reacting how it would biologically after the way he tried to seduce me but why was my heart pounding nervously? Why did a tiny part of me feel bad that he did not have any interest in me and was just teasing me?

This was not good. *Not good at all.*

Liquid dripped between my legs, alerting me of how hornily helpless I was, and my brain strayed and made me think of his lips on mine. God! I hated him, I wished he'd fucking get hit by a truck for riling me up the way he did. I despised him for making me lose control of my own body.

I was still cursing Andrei when his dark-haired and blue-eyed maid knocked on my door and came inside without my permission.

"Boss wants you downstairs for dinner." She didn't wait for my response before giving me her back and heading for the door.

"What is your name?"

She turned around, blue eyes staring back at me. "Maria." Her expression was cold, just like Andrei's and his brothers'. I wondered if Russians naturally had stern faces, or was it just the Russians in the underworld?

"How long have you been working for Andrei?"

She hesitated, making me feel like I was crossing a line by asking. I was just a prisoner, after all, one who was being tormented with horniness. "My papa worked for the boss when I was little." Her soft voice was strained with sadness. "Boss took me in after your papa killed my papa and mama ten years ago."

"Oh dear." A mixture of pity and guilt embraced me. "How old are you?"

"Nineteen," she answered then left the room, leaving me to my thoughts. She was two years younger than I was. I hated my papa so much, but I couldn't imagine losing him when I was only nine, yet he was the reason another child had to grow up without her parents. It broke my heart, that that kind of monster was my papa.

Several minutes passed before I remembered Maria had asked me to come down for dinner. I reluctantly slid out of the bed and checked my hair in the vanity mirror.

The clothes Andrei had gotten for me were still sitting on the table. I wondered if he'd expect me to wear them but decided against it since he'd most likely think I was wearing them to get his attention—which would in fact be true. I resolved that it wouldn't be a good idea and went downstairs wearing my baggy shorts and a sleeveless tee.

Graveyard-level silence covered the house as I went downstairs. The door leading to the dining room was a non-transparent crystal glass. I prayed a short *Hail Mary* before opening it and walking inside.

My eyes were the first to react to the unfamiliar room over-brightened by a golden chandelier that looked like it cost millions of dollars. I narrowed my eyes so they could adjust to the brightness before squinting around and almost letting out a squeal.

I'd always hated blue and now four blue pairs of eyes decided I was the most interesting thing to look at. Three out of the four I'd seen before but one was odd, more friendly than the others, and I assumed they belonged to Andrei's third brother.

The dining table was a standard royal gold shade, long enough for a banquet of fifty people and arranged with enough food to feed the Bronx community. Andrei was sitting at the end of the table, the guy I'd kicked in the balls was sitting by his left and the one who'd led me to Andrei's office with a gun on my waist was sitting beside him. I glared at both of them, letting them see how much I wanted to jump over the table to squeeze their life out of them.

At the right side of the table and two seats away from Andrei was the unfamiliar one with warm eyes. He gave me a smile. "You must be Adrienne."

"Yes," I nodded. "And you are?"

He peered angrily at all his brothers as if they'd all committed a grave sin of some sort. "No one has told you about me?"

"No one has told me about anyone," I said with a shake of my head, giving Andrei my most wicked stare. He was too busy on his phone to even look at me.

"Come, have a seat." The warm-eyed one rose to his feet and pulled the chair beside him out—which was the first chair at Andrei's right hand. "I will introduce everyone to you."

I really didn't want to sit beside Andrei, but I accepted it because I really didn't have a choice; it was obvious the chair was reserved for me. "Thank you," I muttered as I cautiously sat.

"You're welcome," he said, returning to his own chair. "I am Isidor, the youngest." He pointed at the one I'd kicked in the balls. "That one is Alexei, second eldest," then at the one that held his gun at me. "That one is Dimitri, the middle child."

It made sense why middle children are the least loved because I hated the middle one even more than I hated Andrei right now. "Nice to meet you, Isidor," I said genuinely. "Though I can't say the same about your brothers." It was the truth, none of them even tried to look pleasant during the introduction, *cold-hearted bastards.*

"It is rude to be late to dinner," Andrei finally broke his silence without looking up.

I knew it was rude, but I wasn't about to apologize. "What are you going to do about it, pin me against a wall like you did earlier?" It was only after the words left my mouth that I realized what I'd just said.

Everyone's stunned gazes flickered between me and Andrei but they quickly looked away when Andrei peered in each of their directions.

"Either shut up and eat or return to your room," Andrei said brusquely, holding an unreadable expression that made me slightly uncomfortable. As much as I would have preferred to be in a dungeon than sit with three men that had uncanny facial resemblances and personalities like that of the chalcanthite rock, the rumble in my stomach forced me to stay put in my chair. It was either that or I starve to death at night.

"Adrienne," Isidor whispered to me. "Your fists are clenched."

I looked at my hands and my fists were really clenched. I hadn't even noticed. I unclenched them and waited for someone to start filling their plate with food, but it was as if no one wanted to. I ran out of patience, took a flat ceramic serving utensil, and started throwing food on my plate. *Roast beef, stewed potatoes and carrots, mushroom…*

Dimitri was glaring at me as if I'd committed a sin greater than them murdering people. I was indifferent to his spiteful gaze as I started stuffing my mouth.

"Andrei always takes the first bite," Isidor whispered again.

"Well," I replied with my cheeks swollen with stewed potatoes, "he doesn't look like he is ready to eat just yet." Isidor exhaled exhaustingly and I immediately understood. "So, he keeps everyone else starving when he isn't ready to eat?"

I tilted my head to Andrei who was still busy on his phone. What if it was Camilla he was talking to? I shot up from my seat and dragged his phone from him. He glowered at me with complete shock, and I could see Alexei and Dimitri stand up cautiously to defend Andrei from me as if they'd be able to save him if I intended to really kill him.

"Don't you have any manners?" I yelled at Andrei. "You don't use your fucking phone at the table! You can't just keep everyone waiting till you decide you're ready to eat."

Andrei did not say anything in response to my correction, which made me even more upset. "Won't you say something?" I queried.

"Something, like what?"

I scoffed, he had to be the most annoying person in existence. "You're really a heartless bastard."

The calm in his eyes turned into a raging storm. For a minute, the dining room was noiseless while Andrei and I had a cold war on who would look at the other in the cruelest way possible. "Sit down…or I'll press you to the walls until your lungs burst and every bone in your body shatters," he said.

For someone who had a reputation as the cruelest Bratva leader to have ever existed, Andrei had been soft to me so far. I knew I was slowly pushing him beyond his limit, and although I didn't think he'd take his threat all the way, I wasn't willing to push my luck too far. So, I sat.

I'd noticed Isidor tugging on my shorts since I stood. I'd ignored him because I was too busy starting a war I could not win.

"Andrei has never demanded that we do not touch the food when he hasn't," Isidor explained. "We decided to do it to show our respect for him even though he hates it himself."

I just fucked up. "It's still rude to press your phone while at the table with your family," I retorted quietly in defense of my rash behavior.

Andrei ignored me. He stood and then did the most unspeakable thing. He shared the food amongst his brothers. And I noticed as he served himself last.

"What is he doing?" I whispered to Isidor.

"Andrei always makes sure we have enough on our plates," Isidor replied. "He's done that since we were kids."

"Surprising for someone who wouldn't let his brothers eat until he does," I remarked, unwilling to accept how cool Andrei was.

"You're misunderstanding him," Isidor said. "He doesn't let us take the first bite just in case the food isn't safe. Our mother was poisoned, and he's been paranoid ever since."

My jaw fell open. I was dumbstruck now. Andrei wasn't heartless? He cared about his brothers, at least?

It felt surreal to me, perhaps because my own father who had a similar reputation to Andrei wouldn't even blink twice before letting me die in his stead. I really didn't think Andrei would be that different from him. I thought he'd be worse at the very least.

Andrei was seated now. The brothers held each other's hands, bowed their heads, and Andrei said a brief prayer while I watched in awe. They waited for Andrei to take the first bite of his food before they dug into theirs.

"I heard from Alexei you don't wish to manage the hotel in the countryside," Andrei started. "Is there something else you wish to do?"

Isidor cleared his throat. "I haven't thought of anything else for now."

"You know you can't stay partying and fucking around for the rest of your life," Andrei said. "Make a decision within the month and I'll support you if I find it viable."

"Thank you," Isidor said and resumed eating while Andrei talked to Alexei and Dimitri. He was trying to keep up with their personal lives and for some reason, I was almost tearing up. It was good to see that Andrei at least had the ability to be nice and care about something or someone.

Maybe being married to him wasn't going to be as horrible as I thought after all, and I may even shed a tear or two when I killed him. I hoped not to see this side of him more often because I wasn't sure if I'd go on with my plans if I did.

I had to remember Andrei may be good and kind to his brothers, but I wasn't one of them.

We spent the rest of dinner quietly. Alexei and Dimitri were the first to leave the table. Isidor joined later but not without telling me he'd be coming to keep me company sometimes. I thought I should apologize for jumping to conclusions earlier, but I resolved against it because I was the one being held captive here, not him.

I straightened myself from the chair and started for the door when his deep thunderous voice stopped me.

"Adrienne."

I froze because that was the first time he was actually calling me by my name. My heart jumped carelessly because I liked the way he called it; it made me want him. "Yes." My tone was coated with a softness that I didn't even know I had.

"Come here."

My legs started moving to him before my head could process his command. It was at that very moment I realized I was really fucked. My papa would be rolling in brown blood if he came to know the daughter he'd trained so hard to become a son was being a good little girl for the man whose lifeless head he dreamt of having every night.

"Sit."

I wanted to grab a chair, but Andrei grabbed my hand and made me sit on his lap. A thousand butterflies with wings as tough as bats flew in my stomach. Awareness of how close my ass was to Andrei's dick spread around me like wildfire. I was hopeless, my senses gone with my freedom.

"Were you engaged to Mario Luigi?"

My heart switched places with my stomach as I heard that name, and my stomach churned nervously, making me sick and nauseous. Did my papa find out I was with Andrei? Was Andrei going to return me so I could get married to Mario? I didn't want to admit it before but being captive here gave me more peace than being with my papa—not knowing who I had to kill next, who I had to seduce, or when I'd be given a punishment that would destroy my body until I finally gave up.

"Did—" I swallowed fearfully. "Are you taking me back to my papa?" My eyes began to sting as terror gripped me. "I can't go back to him, please." Tears started to roll down my cheeks.

Andrei cleaned my tears away with his bare hands. "*Nyet, malysh.* Didn't I tell you I'm the only one who has the right over you?"

"What do you plan to do? My papa will not sit still when he finds out where I am."

"That is what I want, let him come to me." Andrei put his hands inside my tee and brushed it over my back. It had almost healed and there was barely any pain as his fingers trailed over my skin. "Did he do this to you?"

"Yes," I nodded.

"Was Mario there when it happened?"

More tears filled my eyes and cracked my voice. "He laughed."

Andrei caressed my cheeks, baring his dark-blue eyes into mine. "He won't be laughing the next time he sees a whip."

An eerie feeling crept up my spine with the way Andrei sounded. Darkness clouded every bit of emotion in his voice. Was he going to whip Mario?

Chapter 10 - Adrienne

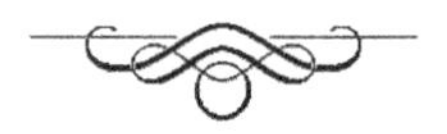

Mornings were my least favorite part of the day. Sometimes, I wished I died in my sleep, and a few times, I'd even wondered what it would feel like swinging down from my ceiling.

Maybe Papa will care. Maybe he will hurt for me and finally look at me with love. Those were my thoughts every morning.

But with each morning I woke up and saw the dread on his face. Every single time he treated me as nothing more than a war dog and a killing machine, I learned something. Papa would not cry for me if I died, he would simply toss my body into a river and if I was lucky enough, he would toss me in with me a nice black casket to keep the sharks away from my lifeless body.

I woke up one morning and I no longer craved his love or for him to treat me like a father would a daughter.

I woke up one morning and I became *morte.*

The sky was still pitch black that morning, but it had been void of stars. I closed my eyes; I could still hear the rough wind whooshing in my window and the footsteps down the hall.

I'd picked up a dagger, a small dagger my papa gifted me after he killed my pet bunny on my tenth birthday. It was still smeared with dried blood, and I hadn't touched it before then.

But I grabbed it from the box where I'd hidden it away and tiptoed into the hallway. I saw a figure enter my papa's room, so I followed it.

Some of the memories of that day had faded but I remembered my papa's shout. I ran into the room without thinking and before I knew it, I'd slashed the man's throat.

My dagger had hit him straight in the carotid artery and he was dead in a matter of minutes. I was trembling inside, scared that I'd just killed a man, but when I looked up and saw the proud smile on my papa's face, I tightened my grip on the dagger.

I knew right there and then that someday, my papa would die by that dagger.

A knock on my door brought me back to the present. I whipped my head around just as someone opened the door and entered. It was Maria and she was holding a white gown.

"What the hell is that?"

She laid it on the bed beside me. "The boss asked me to help you wear it."

I laughed because I couldn't believe it. Everything felt surreal. Not too long ago, I was planning my papa's death, today, I'm in Andrei's house and about to be his bride. I shuddered just thinking of it.

"Take that piece of trash back to him and tell him I won't be attending our wedding."

Maria didn't move.

"Did you hear what I said?"

She looked up at me, and it was almost as if she was glaring at me. "You have to do as the boss says or…"

"I won't do as he says, tell him I said that."

Maria sighed. "If you don't put this on, the boss will hurt you. He will break you and destroy your spirit. He will crush you."

I stared at her in disbelief. "What did you just say to me?"

She looked down at the ground. "I'm sorry." The words came out forced. "I'm only trying to keep you safe from the boss."

Something was wrong with Maria; I didn't know what it was, but she seemed strange. Maria wasn't my problem, though, this shitty marriage with Andrei was, so I grabbed the dress from the bed and skedaddled out of the room.

I ran down the stairs and to the foyer, screaming, "Andrei! Come out here you fucker!" I was seeing red and couldn't get myself to think straight. "Where the fuck are you, Andrei? I'm burning this house down if you don't get your pervert ass out here."

I panted, my blood boiling with rage. I could use my dagger right now, really.

"The priest will be here any moment." Andrei's voice came from the stairs, so I tilted my head up to look at him. "You should get dressed."

I laughed like I was crazy because I was certain I'd really gone insane. "Get dressed?" I started to rip the dress apart, biting it, chewing it, all while screaming and laughing maniacally.

Andrei didn't try to stop me. He stood on the stairs watching me with a displeased look on his face which was exactly what I wanted.

"Fuck you!" I screamed as I ripped a part of the dress with my bare hands. "If you want a bride that badly then you can become one yourself."

Satisfied with the damage I'd done to the dress, I tossed it to him and it landed just in front of the banister he was leaning on. I smiled victoriously. "Now, what did you say about us getting married?" I panted.

Andrei wouldn't have any choice but to cancel the wedding, and I thought I'd get him to cancel a couple more till he changed his mind and decide that marrying me wasn't the best course of action.

I peered straight at him as he climbed down the stairs. His face had no expression and for some reason, my stomach knotted in fear. I'd acted rashly. I'd given in to my impulsive thoughts without thinking of the possible consequences of doing so.

Was Andrei going to hurt me? I knew he was capable of doing it but was he going to kill me?

My heart started racing in my chest, but I tried not to show it. I couldn't let him see how intimidated he'd made me feel.

"Pick it up." His was serious and terrifying. The bass in it made it even more intimidating than the scowl growing on his face.

I swallowed. "No."

"Haven't I told you, *malysh*? No one says no to me."

"Well, I'm not sorry things are no longer that way for you."

Andrei barred his teeth and raked his hand through his hair, exasperated. "Do it while I'm being nice."

I knew he was furious, but something in me pushed me to test him further. I wanted to drive him over the edge and see how far his anger could go. "No."

Andrei spun around with speed, grabbed my neck, and before I could register what was happening, I was pinned against the wall.

Was he going to hit me? I scoffed. I'd gotten used to being beaten up, this was nothing.

Andrei didn't hit me, but he did something worse. He slid his hand beneath my dress and started to tease my clitoris.

It was so good I wanted to moan, but I didn't, I couldn't let him know I was enjoying his torture. I didn't want to encourage his behavior.

"When I tell you to do something, you do it." He removed his hand and moved away from me. "Dress up and come outside if you don't wish to be shipped to Mario instead."

Exactly an hour later, I was dressed in a white dress that looked like it had decayed in a trash can. It was ripped all over and I was so pale, I looked like the corpse bride.

The damn dress wasn't even decent enough to cover my shame.

Truthfully, I'd thought I'd seen Maria smile mockingly at me when I climbed down the stairs, but I'd been imagining it. I honestly wouldn't blame her if she laughed though, I looked horrible and this fucking thing on my body was laughable. I would've laughed if I wasn't the one getting married in rags.

I hadn't worn this dress because I was afraid of Andrei, I'd worn it because, for some reason, I preferred being Andrei's hostage rather than Mario's animal.

Andrei smiled at me when I reached the patio, and I rolled my eyes at him. I wondered if he knew how much I wanted to play Russian roulette with my pistol pointed at his head. The fucker probably knew, but he definitely underestimated me.

Ego was a common disease with men in our world. They thought too highly of themselves and too little of women.

They always learned from their mistakes, but it was almost always too late when they did.

A white-haired priest stood at the end of the patio. He looked way into his sixties, and I could see he was struggling really hard not to look at me.

"You look charming," Andrei said, mocking me with his eyes.

I looked him over from head to toe. "You look terrible," I muttered. He didn't. If anything, he looked so good that my gaze lingered on him longer than I wanted it to.

His black suit struggled to contain his large shoulders and he looked really good in it. If I didn't hate him as much as I did, I would've even gone ahead to call him 'handsome.'

He smelled so good too and I wanted to close my eyes and take in his rosewood smell.

"Is this her?" the priest asked. I could pick up the Russian in his accent and he was looking at me like I was a sinner he was ready to condemn to death.

Andrei dipped his head in a nod.

The priest cleared his throat and gave me a side eye to show his disgust. He was probably thinking I was an Italian whore who wasn't worthy of marrying a murderous, blood-thirsty mafia boss.

"Please face each other, I shall start now."

Andrei and I turned, our eyes glued on each other. I wondered what he was thinking but I hoped he wasn't thinking of consummating this fake marriage. I would just kill him them.

A vivid memory of him rubbing my clitoris sent a shiver of electricity all over my body and my clit pulsated to it.

I almost enjoyed his touch. *Almost.* But I didn't. Whatever was happening in between my legs right now was my body being a body and misunderstanding what had happened.

The priest went on to mutter nonsense like talking about how a man who finds a wife finds a good thing and I tried to resist the urge to ask if that applied to a man who kidnapped a wife.

Because I sure as hell wasn't going to make Andrei's life peaceful.

"Are you here out of your own volition?" the priest asked, looking at me. I found his question really offensive considering he most certainly knew I wasn't.

I stared at Andrei and then back at the priest. "Cut the crap, you already know I'm not."

The old priest blinked at Andrei, his downturned eyes filled with confusion. "What does this mean?"

Andrei shot a glare my way and I returned it with one of my own. "Forgive me, Father. My fiancée is insufferable."

Can you blame her?

"Common, *malysh,*" Andrei said, opening his blazer. It took a while for me to see the gun in his inner pocket. "Let's not do this in front of the priest."

The distraught look wrinkling the priest's face made it evident he had no idea.

Was he really going to shoot me on our wedding day? I'd envisioned many ways I could die, and dying in a rag-looking white dress with a Russian staring down at me wasn't one of them.

I wanted to die with honor and be remembered for the gift I'll give the other girls in the world—a gift of being the one to kill Dante Paolo for his ruthlessness. There'll be fewer missing girls when I do that.

Fewer young girls would end up missing for no reason if I succeeded.

We exchanged our vows, and I was more than happy to say, "'til death do us part." I couldn't wait until that day.

Andrei slid a golden band with an enormous diamond at the center of it into my finger. It was beautiful and shiny. I'd never thought of getting married. I'd never imagined myself being bound to anyone.

"It looks beautiful on you," he said, as if we were a real couple. I cringed, flinging my hand away from him.

"I wish I could say the same about you." I slid another plain gold ring onto his ring finger. "Sadly, even a gold ring can't beautify a pig."

Andrei snorted, laughing at a joke made simply to humiliate him. "I love your sense of humor, *malysh.*"

I could've vomited. Instead, I was frozen in time as I watched Andrei laugh. Something about the way his lips spread and the way his dark eyes sparkled warmed my heart and settled a sizzle in my stomach. He looked beautiful, too handsome for a cold-blooded killer.

"One day, you will think of me as more than a pig. You'll need me and beg for me."

Just hearing him talk disintegrated the sizzle in my stomach. He was really likable until he opened his mouth. "Your voice is aggravating."

"Yours makes me want to hear you moan."

I opened my mouth, ready to attack him, but closed it when the priest broke into our conversation. I'd almost forgotten he was here. "If there's any reason why this marriage should not happen, this is the time to speak up."

There were lots of reasons why this marriage shouldn't happen and absolutely no reason why it should.

But I kept my lips sealed when Andrei smiled at me, massaging the part of his jacket where his gun was safely hidden. And a feeble old Russian priest wouldn't be of much help to me anyway.

"I now pronounce you, husband and wife." The corner of the priest's lips wrinkled into a smile. "You may kiss your bride."

Andrei leaned in and I shut my eyes. *Maybe I should bite his lips when he comes close enough for me to.*

He did come close enough to perch a light kiss on my lips. *Gross.*

Then he leaned in toward my ear. "Did you hear that, *malysh?*" he said in a whisper. "You are now officially mine.

Chapter 11 - Andrei

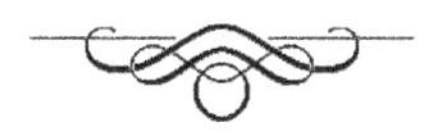

"Didn't I tell you, *malysh?*" I moved closer to her, expecting her to pace back, but she didn't. "You're mine. Mine to torment, mine to punish, and mine to *touch.*"

Adrienne sneered at me, her beautiful gray eyes sparking with mischief. "You're really a nutjob, aren't you?" She folded her hands over her chest. "I'm not an item, Andrei. I do not belong to you."

She walked to her bed and sank down on it, looking away from me.

Did she know how much her stubbornness turned me on? If she did, she wouldn't try to argue with me. She would've tried to do as I said.

It'd been almost two hours since we got married. Two hours since I forced her to say *I do.*

After I leaned closer to her ear and marked her as mine, goosebumps spread across her skin and I heard her little yelp.

Adrienne was scared of me. I could see it despite how hard she tried to hide it, and I was glad she tried really hard to.

The last thing I wanted was a little white-haired Italian woman cowering with fear whenever she saw me.

Many people thought I was ruthless—*I think I am too*—yet I hated being feared, or maybe I just hated Adrienne fearing me.

What fun would all of this be if my sweet little *malysh* winced away whenever I walked close to her? I had no intention of finding out because I preferred it this way.

Her smart mouth did a lot of things to me. She made me as angry as she made me hard.

Her little fit before our wedding this afternoon was a good example. Her display of madness had sent blood rushing to my dick. I'd been hard. I'd wanted to throw her against the wall and bury my cock inside her at that moment.

Fuck. Even now, I wanted to fuck her. I wanted to transform her furious yell into moans. I wanted to choke her while fucking her from behind.

I could barely control myself right now and she was instigating me to touch her with her stubbornness. My *malysh* would learn sooner or later that misbehaving wasn't going to do her any good.

"I do not fucking belong to you!" She screamed at the top of her voice.

"You're wrong, *malysh*. You do."

She breathed. "Forget making me an item. What do you wish to do now?" she asked. "I'm certain you didn't insist on marrying me just to keep me hostage forever and force me to birth little Russian spawns with your face."

"You're right, I didn't marry you just so you can have my children." Although I wouldn't mind if she did. I needed an heir to continue this bloody business after I die.

"Our deal is sealed now, tell me everything about your father."

She whipped her head toward me. "And Mario?"

Right, Mario. I had plans for that imbecile. Deadly plans.

It was hard to imagine his laughing face while my *malysh* suffered. I'd never wanted anything else the way I wanted to punish him.

I wanted to see him on his knees, begging to be spared, promising never to laugh again. I wanted him to kneel before Adrienne.

And I knew she wanted it too, but there was only one problem. Adrienne wouldn't want me to kill him. She would want me to punish him, break him, and then have mercy on him.

I didn't believe in mercy though, or perhaps I didn't believe in her definition of mercy. I believed death was mercy, but I never gave assholes like him a clean death either.

I tortured them, made them bleed. I made their mercy painful because it was their punishment too.

"Mario will pay for what he did to you, I assure you of that," I replied.

"My father is into a lot of shady businesses. You're familiar with most of them since you're into them yourself."

I narrowed my eyes at her. "There are lots of shady businesses in the cartel, but there are hierarchies to them." I did whatever needed to be done, but child and human trafficking were where I drew the line.

Was I still a bastard? Probably. But a bastard with a code of honor was better than one without it.

"Don't fool yourself into thinking you're any better than him. You're not."

"I never said I was." I moved from the doorframe to the bed and sat down on the edge beside her. "But I think you know there's a difference between me and your papa. You wouldn't have come to me if you didn't think so."

"The only difference between the two of you is who dies first. You're both misogynists with no regard for women or their lives."

She wasn't entirely wrong, but she wasn't entirely right either.

I had opinions some would consider misogynist. Opinions like how our dark underworld was not fitting for women.

But that was simply because they were the most endangered. I'd seen how men treated them. It didn't matter if they were their mothers, sisters, or wives. Those animals just wanted to trample on them.

Adrienne and her mother were proof of that.

"I agree," I said because it didn't matter what I told her, she wouldn't believe me. "Now back to your papa."

"There's nothing more I can tell you, not until I am certain my head won't be dismembered from the rest of my body after you get what you want."

I nodded. She was right to not want to become collateral damage in our fight, and I had no problems with her holding onto something she could negotiate with.

Even though I had no intention of hurting her…or ever letting her go.

Adrienne knew nothing about me other than the absurd pictures her papa had painted in her head of who I was. She didn't know a thing about my possessive nature.

Once I wanted something, I made sure to get it.

After I get what I want, I never let it go.

"If that is all then leave my room," she commanded. "I'm exhausted and my lips hurt from making vows I have no intention of keeping."

There she was, taunting me again.

"Don't tell me you're thinking of consummating this marriage, you know I wouldn't let you do that."

She was rejecting me with her words, but the blush on her cheeks was saying something entirely different.

Adrienne wanted me, even more than I wanted her. The way her pussy clenched when I glided my finger into it said enough. She'd been so wet, and a moan had even escaped her throat.

The only reason why I was holding myself back was because I wanted her to beg for me. I wanted her to want me so much that she wouldn't care about her ego.

I would fuck only then.

That didn't mean I couldn't touch her, torment her, or tease her how I wanted. I would until her wall crumbles and she would have no choice but need me to quell the dirty desires I'd built inside her.

"We're married, and I'm certain you know we must consummate our marriage tonight."

Her cheeks turned crimson and her eyes dilated. She licked her lips and swallowed, trying to calm herself.

Oh, my poor, little malysh. She had no idea what was awaiting her.

I smiled to myself because she didn't even know how much effect I had on her already, and it would be too late by the time she realized it.

Because by then, I would've infiltrated her mind and thoughts until there was nothing left but longing and need for me. I would use her feelings as leverage to get to that rat, Dante Paolo.

I would get everything I could on him and then hit him where it hurts the most. I could already envision the shock on his face when he finds out I used his own daughter against him. A daughter he mistreated all her life.

That would be the start of his punishment.

"Do you believe this is a marriage?" she raged. "Why weren't your brothers there? If you really believed this was a real marriage, then you should've let them be there with us."

I'd stopped my brothers from attending the wedding for good reason. Alexei had no interest in being there while I married an Italian woman he hated. He and Dimitri had an important task of finding out all they can about Mario by tonight, and Isidor hadn't answered my call for a day now.

Who knows what trouble he is causing now?

"My brothers didn't need to be there. I'm the one you were getting married to, not them." I stood up, took her hand, and dragged her up with me. "*Malysh,* I'm your husband and you need to speak to me with more respect, don't you think?"

"If you needed a submissive wife, then you shouldn't have married a killer."

"Good point," I agreed. "But what fun is there if I marry a woman groomed to be the perfect wife? I prefer to tame my women myself."

My dick was straining painfully against my zipper now. God, I wasn't sure how much longer I could wait for her to accept me. I pinned her against the wall and sniffed her hair, taking in the scent of her strawberry shampoo.

"You smell so good," I groaned, pressing my waist into hers so she could feel how hard she was making me. "You feel so good."

Adrienne tried to struggle free, but I held her in place. "You have to behave, wife. Your struggles are turning me on."

"I'm not your wife," she panted. "And I'll chop your cock off before I even dream of fucking you."

I tucked a lock of white hair behind her ear. "Deny it all you want, but you know the truth and you can't escape it."

She was palpitating. It made me smile seeing how determined she was to not show me the emotions she knew I wanted her to. And it was even funnier seeing how badly she was failing at it.

"Andrei..."

"Shh." I placed a finger on her lips. It was soft, velvety, and I wanted to know what it tastes like. I hovered my tongue on her lips, keeping her warm with the heat radiating from my body. "Do you want me to kiss you, *malysh?*"

She didn't give an answer immediately, but I knew what the answer would be. She was biting her lips and moving her legs. I knew she was wet. How wet she was became a mystery I wanted to solve.

"I don't," she finally replied, lying through her teeth.

"Are you saying the truth?" I licked her neck. "Will you really not be wet if I put a finger inside your cunt right now."

She gasped. "I won't."

"Liar," I groaned. "I know you want me. I know your cunt is weeping for my touch. I know your clitoris is pulsating, waiting for me to bless it with my finger and my tongue."

She opened her mouth as if she wanted to object but closed it back up. Words failed her. She settled with shaking her head.

I ripped the ball of her white dress apart and glided my fingers between her thighs. She jerked, her breath raspy.

My cock was straining against the zipper of my suit now. It was hard and needy for my sweet little Adrienne. But it had to wait. *Not yet.*

Adrienne patted her legs to grant my wandering hands more freedom. She wanted me to satisfy the weight between her legs, and I was going to do anything but that. I wasn't even going to kiss her yet.

"Do you know all the things I want to do to you?"

She swallowed loudly. "I don't care."

A wicked grin itched the back of my throat. "Yes, you do," I whispered. "You want to hear all the ways I can make you scream, you want to know the different positions I'll put you in while I fuck you."

I pressed my waist into hers a little further. "Can you feel it?" I asked. "Can you feel how hard I am?" I greased the folding of her pussy with my fingers. "I want to fuck you right now, little wife, and I want you to scream my name while I do it."

I leaned in as if I wanted to kiss her and she closed her eyes, ready to receive my kiss. But I didn't kiss her. "I want to fuck you, but I won't. You haven't earned it yet."

She opened her eyes and pushed me away. Her push was light, not enough to move me one bit. I paced back, letting her think she'd actually set herself free from me. "Is it fun teasing me, asshole?"

"It is," I answered. While I'd have loved to tease her a little more, I had other things to do. "See you later, *malysh.*"

I turned around and started for the door. Pulling my phone out from my pocket, I dialed Alexei's number. "Is it done?"

"Yes. I traced him to his house."

I wasn't an unromantic guy, although I hadn't been involved with anyone I needed to please. Today was my wedding day with Adrienne and I needed to give her a gift. One she would be more than happy to receive.

"Get the boys ready, we leave at dawn."

CHAPTER 12 - ADRIENNE

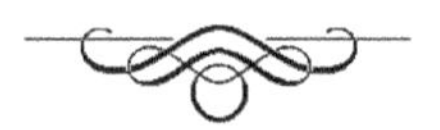

The same nightmare had hunted me since I was a child; a woman with a face like my own staring back at me, a man with a voice like my papa's roaring, screams from a voice I was not familiar with, and the sound of my own voice crying.

It always felt the same whenever I woke from the nightmare. My body was always wet with sweat, my heart pounding as if it wanted to explode, and I had this feeling that it wasn't just a dream.

Deep voices and footsteps came from downstairs. I remembered falling asleep after Andrei humiliated me and left the room.

That man had an effect on me that I didn't like one bit. A single touch from him evoked so much emotion in me and he knew it. I knew he was baiting me, making me go crazy for him until he decided it was time to devour me.

Yet, I couldn't resist him. I wanted to, but I couldn't.

I'd been so wet, and he would have discovered that if he'd stayed back to touch me a little more. Goddamnit! I was even wet right now just thinking of him. I'd tried to touch myself to ease the tension he'd created in me, but it just wasn't enough.

Imagining him wasn't what I needed. Him whispering dirty words into my ears and taking care of my needs was what I really needed.

Believe me, I knew how stupid I sounded, wanting a man I needed dead to fuck me. I put my bottom lips between my tongue and bit hard on it to escape the crazy thoughts in my head and bring myself back to reality.

I peeked out of the window and the sky was still pitch black, dazzling with stars and a half-crescent moon. I sighed. I'd been nine the last time I cared to admire nature.

I didn't have a phone and there was no clock in my room for me to tell the time but seeing as it was still dark outside, I knew it wasn't morning yet.

The ruckus downstairs continued. I decided to find out what is wrong myself. I descended the stairs lightly, deliberately not to give away my presence. It was a technique I learned growing up because in this dark world of ours, you could never tell when your enemies would have it out for you.

And unfortunately for me, I had enemies on every side. My papa's enemies and Andrei's, considering I was now a prisoner of his—which many would understand to mean that I was now married to him.

My rapid breaths steadied when I reached the base of the stairs to find Andrei, Alexei, Dimitri, and Andrei's men standing in the foyer. Andrei was wearing a white dress shirt with what appeared to be an artwork of red ink, except it wasn't red ink. It was blood.

I ran down to stairs and grabbed him by the arm, examining him for injuries while asking myself why I cared if he was injured. Andrei meant nothing to me, that was what I believed, but why was I here making a fool of myself and checking if he was wounded? *Why?*

Was I afraid to become a widow as quickly as I became a wife? I shook the question off. That wasn't it. I didn't care if Andrei lived or died. I settled with the thought that I just didn't want him dead until I'd gotten my revenge.

That was it.

"*Malysh.*" He removed my two hands from his shirt and looked down at me. A part of his face was also stained with blood. "You'll get your pretty hands dirty."

"It doesn't matter how dirty I get my hands; I need to make certain your fine." I sounded like a fool saying that, but I didn't have the time to cringe at my own words.

I reached to touch him again, but he held me back. "I am fine, *malysh.*" He collected a black trash bag from one of his men and handed it to me.

I perceived a pungent metallic tang from the bag, and it was heavy to carry. "What is inside?" I asked. Maybe I was a coward, but I was feeling too hesitant to look inside myself.

Andrei's lips twisted into an evil grin, his eyes filled with gloom and a devilish glimmer. "Mario Luigi."

The bag fell out of my hands instantly and landed on the marble floor with a thud. Proving Andrei was not lying and there was indeed a human or at least a human part inside the trash bag. "What?"

In slow motion, I opened the bag to see what part Andrei had chosen to hand me as a souvenir. I gasped as my eyes met Mario's old, lifeless brown eyes. Blood was pouring out from his ears and nose, making my stomach churn. I was certain I'd vomit if I looked a little longer, so I tied the bag. "What the fuck, Andrei?"

I was mad at him, very mad. He needed to understand that although I was forced into this dirty world where having a heart was a disease, I was growing a particular dislike to the sight of mutilated bodies, especially a head dismembered from the rest of the body. I gave him my most irritated frown.

"What is it?" He tried to touch my cheeks with his bloody hands my I moved my head to evade his touch.

"Why did you do this?"

Andrei looked around, signaling the other guys to give us privacy before responding. "What did I do?"

"This!" I screamed, pointing at the trash bag. "You could have just killed him, why did you have to cut him like that?"

"Because that was what you wanted."

"That wasn't what I wanted," I retorted. "This isn't what I want, Andrei. This brutal killing, it isn't what I want."

"What do you want?" That was the first time in my existence that someone asked me that question, and now I wasn't even sure what I wanted anymore. I'd come here with the intention of using Andrei and killing him afterward, but now it seemed like I wanted something different.

"What do you want, *malysh?*" The question came to me very coldly, demanding. He yanked my hair back and a moan escaped my throat. "I'll tell you what I want." His stare spread all over my body like fire would spread through cotton. "I want to kill everyone who has hurt you, I want to gift you their fucking heads and watch you trample over their corpses."

"That's the fucking problem, Andrei." My breath was ragged from the heat filling the room, my head still thrown back from his tight grip. "I'm not a monster like you, I don't want heads and corpses."

"Tell me." He moved so close that the blood on his shirt was smearing on my skin, the hotness of his body melting me. "Tell me what it is you want."

"I want you dead." I didn't know if that was even the truth anymore. "I fucking want you and every other bastard like you dead."

Intense darkness seeped into Andrei's eyes. "Guess what, sweetie?" His words came out like a bare whisper. "I am hard to kill."

He tossed my hair away, making me lose my balance and fall to the ground. He lowered himself to a squat, brushing a bloody thumb on my lips. "There are many things you do not know, many things."

"Maybe there are." I shook my head to fling his fingers away from my lips. "But I do not want you close to me. You're fucking disgusting." I didn't know that I wanted to say those terrible things to him. I hated that I wanted to see to this man's death myself. I hated that he'd just gone ahead and killed someone for me. I hated it even more that a part of me liked what he did, and that part of me wanted to pull his bloodstained body in and kiss him. Maybe I was a monster after all, maybe I was just like my papa and every other bloodsucker in New York.

Andrei's gaze lingered on me before he erected himself. "I'll bathe, then we talk."

"There is nothing to talk about," I yelled after him. He didn't turn around or give a response and he disappeared from my view, leaving me alone in the foyer. The ground felt hard and the cold trailed its way to my ears, muffling the pounding of my heart. I stood, straightened myself up, and ambled to my room, taking the stairs two at a time.

What the fuck was that? I closed the door behind me and leaned on it, regret and guilt pouring over me as I thought of the things I said to Andrei. I'd taken out my ill emotions on him but truthfully, he was not the person I was mad at, it was my papa for dragging me into this mess of a world. I was also mad at myself because, for the first time, I looked at a dead man's head and felt a creep of satisfaction, I looked at a ruthless murderer and wanted to give him my most thankful smile.

I was messed up, more than I actually liked to believe.

My reflection stared back at me from the mirror in the vanity, blood smeared on my lips, darkness over my grey eyes, and a tee that made me look like the Elm Street murderer. Had I always looked so much like my papa?

I pulled the tee over my head, dragged down my baggy shorts, and headed to the shower. There was a very slim chance bathing would wash away the version of myself I'd always denied having existed, but I was willing to take any chance I had.

Warm water beat calmly on my skin, washing away the dried blood that formed a red pool around my feet. Different thoughts filled my head. I'd let myself get distracted in just a few days, only God knew what my papa was up to, and I had to do something before he found me—that's if he didn't know where I was already. It was either I go ahead with my plan and take my papa down before he had a chance to drag me back to his manor, or I made a perfect excuse for my disappearance.

I chose the latter.

Turned out Andrei was more of a problem to me than I thought he would be. I'd let him crawl under my skin and couldn't afford to lose focus. My life and the lives of many other women who would be kidnapped, trafficked, and heaven knows what else depended on what I'd planned to do next.

I turned off the shower and padded into the bedroom Andrei had chosen to be my prison. The bag of clothes he'd gotten for me was still carefully sitting on the vanity. I walked over to it and took out the clothes to choose which of them would be the best to murder someone in.

One of the black dresses caught my eye. I held it up to get a full view of it. One look and I decided it was the perfect dress for the night, a slit dress with an exposed back. The bodice was nothing but gold chains and I was sure it wouldn't do a good enough job of covering my 40D cup breasts. I guess it wasn't a bad idea for a man to die with his eyes firmly on my nipples.

That was what my papa trained me to be anyway, *a seductress who brings death to men.*

Five minutes later I was wearing the dress that fit as if it was made just for me. I'd brushed my hair and done my usual smoky eyes and red lip with makeup items I found in the cupboard of the vanity. I couldn't tell why my breath had clipped a little when I found those makeup items, and it wasn't because I wondered how many women Andrei had held captive in this red room—at least that I was sure of.

There weren't any heels in the shopping bags so I compromised by walking barefoot, just the way I did when I went to Andrei's club five days ago.

I made a straight line for the kitchen as soon as I left my room. It was quiet as if this was a graveyard of some sort, but even graveyards had the sound of swooshing breeze, rustling from dry leaves, and crickets.

But here, it was nothing, as if this building was void of life.

A set of black-headed knives arranged in a knife holder sat on the white kitchen counter when I walked in. It was the first time I'd entered the kitchen since I woke up here. I picked the smallest knife from the set—the smallest were always the sharpest—and left the kitchen.

Andrei's room was just across the hall. I could hear the splash of water from his shower as soon as I opened the door and walked inside. The bloody shirt he'd worn earlier was lying on the floor.

His room was everything I'd not expected a devil's room to be, *white.* From his ceiling to his bed covers, and the recliner across the room. Even the marble floor, walls, and drapes were white. I came to two conclusions, either he was sick in the head enough to give himself the white room torture, or he was a germaphobe.

For someone who was very comfortable with blood on his skin, the chance of him being more messed up in the head was more likely.

I glanced at the part of his room where his closet was and something caught my eye, something made my blood clot, causing the knife to drop with a *clang* to the floor.

A woman with my face and eyes smiled back at me from a black and white portrait on the wall. I covered my hand over my mouth as tears ran down my face.

"Looking for something?"

I spun around in the direction of Andrei's deadly deep voice. His raven hair was wet and curly, dripping water down his broad shoulders and athletic chest that was covered fully with tattoos—he was sexy in a very dark way. My heart sank to my clitoris, making it throb, but that soon faded away when I noticed writing on his left chest right where the heart was located, *Adrienne,* my name was written on his chest.

Why the hell did he have my name written on himself?

The brusque glare in Andrei's eyes screamed he hated how I'd trespassed into his space, and worse, I'd found something I should never have.

Fuck.

Chapter 13 - Andrei

I found it quite odd how repelled Adrienne was by the sight of blood considering she'd had it covering half of her face the first time we met. I'd even thought she'd be more pleased if it was the blood of that fucking raccoon who had the guts to laugh at her to her face.

I'd had him tied to a chair and tickled till his eyes turned crimson with tears and his lungs almost ran out of air before cutting his tongue out like he fucking deserved. I had no regret, even if Adrienne thought otherwise. I'd be quite satisfied killing a hundred more men who dared to cause her pain.

Dante Paolo included.

Footsteps padded into my room just as I was about to turn off the shower, I picked my .45 from the phone holder by the wall and threw a towel around my waist before leaving the bathroom. I'd not bothered to turn off the shower; in situations like this, it was better to let the intruder think you weren't aware of their presence.

A clang sound came from the room as soon as I was able to open the bathroom door without making any sound, and I saw a knife on the floor. Adrienne was standing across the room staring at something close to my closet. I heaved a sigh in relief and tucked my gun behind my back, steadying it with the towel on my waist.

No one had worn the dress she was wearing for twenty years, and even before that, I hadn't thought anyone could be that beautiful in a dress like that one.

Seeing Adrienne in my room like this, with that dress showing off the shape of her round ass, was enough to drive me insane. I wondered if this woman knew the kind of effect she had over me. What was she thinking coming into my room, dressed like a dirty little slut? All I could think of was spanking her ass and ripping off the chains covering her breast.

My cock became alive, erect and pointing itself at her. My brain forgot how to function normally, and I swear I couldn't peel my eyes away from her, not when she was there looking like a snack. *Dammit!* I hated snacks, but Adrienne was a pot of milky chocolate I was ready to fill myself inside.

I tried to make myself sound as indifferent as possible when I asked her if there was something she was looking for, but when she turned and looked at me with misty-puppy eyes, I felt an odd need to comfort her, *or kill for her again.*

"Who is she?" Her voice broke as she demanded an answer from me. "And why does she—"

Fuck me! I'd forgotten to take down the picture from the wall. I pondered what she'd make out of the situation. What were the odds that she'd think I was a stalker or that I was obsessed with her? Either way, it was a more welcome assumption than letting her know the truth.

"Who does she look like?" I'd never had a problem sounding like the king of the abyss himself, but my tone instinctively softened whenever I was talking to her.

Adrienne took a step closer to me, her eyes boring into mine as if she could somehow get an answer from them. "Did you—have you been watching me all this time?"

There was no way I was telling her the truth, but I didn't intend to lie to her either. "What if I was?"

"You've been stalking me before we met at the club?" Her voice edged with anger as if she was merely managing to keep herself from giving into her rage and exploding. "You've been lying to me."

"I haven't lied to you." *I've only kept some details away from you.*

"Meeting me at the club twice, was it all your plan?"

She was making assumptions, trying to get answers from me and for some reason, I wanted to pacify her and make her understand it wasn't what she was thinking.

"God, no." My gaze trailed to her feet; they looked like she'd danced in a pit of fire with naked feet before. "Your question should be directed at someone else."

"I think you are that someone," she retorted. "Why the fuck is my picture here and my name tattooed on your chest?"

I wished I could open up to her, tell her about her mother, about everything. But she'd be in too much pain if I did, so I said the only thing that felt right to say in that moment. "Return to your room, Adrienne. Never come in here again."

A demented kind of chuckle filled the room, her eyes dim with tears and hatred. "I should have killed you when I had the chance to." She picked up the knife on the floor that she'd dropped and brought it to my chest.

Sharp piercing pain was followed by the dripping of blood on my floor.

Chapter 14 - Adrienne

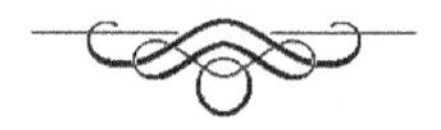

I'd always thought men like Andrei were somehow immune to pain, but now that his blood was dripping on the floor, and his eyes were flickering with fury and...*pain,* I couldn't escape being trapped in my own conscience.

Truth is, I hadn't intended to stab him, I'd thought he would move away before the knife reached him. He didn't, and blood was dripping down his chest, the part where my name was inked on.

It wasn't the right time to note something like this, but he looked like the painting of the hottest demon in hell.

The *drip, drip* as crimson liquid fell to the floor was the only thing heard in the room for the seconds after I cut him. My nerves were working up, making me anxious. I knew I'd crossed a line. What Andrei would do to me now could only be left to my imagination.

And I wasn't going to apologize.

"You really shouldn't have, *malysh.*" He grabbed the knife from me and tossed it across the room, smearing the floor further with red. His jaws twitched and his eyes gloomed violently.

The next thing I felt was strong warm hands wrapping firmly around my neck, making it hard for me to breathe. I placed my hands on his arms, scratching, kicking, and fighting, trying to get his grip loose from my neck but it was futile; I only ran out of breath more quickly than I anticipated.

Andrei wasn't blinking. I'd heard wild bloodthirsty beasts became thoughtless when they saw their own blood, and here I was experiencing it for the first time. I tried to mutter his name, but it only turned into a bubble that flew away with the wind.

I didn't know I was crying until I saw the drop of tears on Andrei's hand. My sight became clouded and my head started to spin. He must've noticed because he ungripped me and threw me on his king-sized bed that looked like clouds without the skies.

I started coughing, desperate to get oxygen into my lungs.

Andrei transferred his aggression to the wall, punching it and repeating, "fuck" as he did. Then he glared at me, the poison from his eyes an undiluted venom on my skin. "Run, Adrienne."

Did I hear him right? I peered at him, arching my brows to show my confusion.

"Run," he repeated with a growl. "Don't let me catch you."

I glanced at the door; he was closer to it, and I was certain I had no chance of getting to it before he caught me. Still, I sprinted out of the bed and ran to the door. I'd only managed to get a few meters away from Andrei's room when he grabbed me by my hair.

"You weren't fast enough, *malysh*." Twisted amusement lurked in his voice, seeping through his hands on my hair and seeping into my bloodstream, raising the speed of my pulse. He dragged me back into the room and flung me so hard on the bed I thought I'd cracked a bone; he locked the door while holding a devilish grin at me.

"What the fuck are you doing?" I gasped, raising myself on all fours. "Let me out, now!"

Andrei walked to me, watching me with sick curiosity. Blood was no longer dripping down his chest, yet I couldn't take my eyes off it. Andrei was probably the type of guy to box every day, and it paid off well enough with how hard his abs looked, his torso was a V-shape, and the tattoo on his chest made him ten times hotter.

I hoped I was imagining the bulging between his legs. *Damn you, Adrienne.* I should've been looking for a way to escape this man, not making love with him in my head.

"On your knees alone, *malysh*," he commanded as he reached the bed. Every will to disobey him vanished when he added, "Now," his Russian accent slipping.

Like the good little girl he loved to call me, I removed my hands from the bed and straightened my back, so I was kneeling like a whore in front of her master.

He cupped my face hard. "You should be punished." I hadn't registered what he meant by "punished" until he yanked my legs and dragged me down, holding me still with one hand and rummaging through his nightstand with the other. He brought out handcuffs and cuffed me to the bed.

"What are you doing?" A mixture of fear and desire laced in my voice.

"Punishing you." He went over to the drawer on the other side of the bed and inserted a blue device on his finger. It was only when he came back to me, turned on the device, and slid his hand into my pussy did I know what it was. I'd heard of finger vibrators before, just never seen one.

His finger, vibrating inside me with that thing on, sent electricity up my spine. The walls inside my pussy tickled in the sweetest way possible while funny noises escaped my throat in response. I wasn't supposed to feel this way, I wasn't supposed to enjoy what he was doing to me.

I gripped the bed tight to keep myself from moaning. "Stop, please," I yelped, unsure of if I really wanted him to. God.

"Are you going to be a good little girl, Adrienne?"

Fuck. He had to call my name like that at a time like this, his Russian accent making my senses seep away from me. "Stop," was the only thing I could bring myself to say amidst the grunt I was biting my lips to hold back.

Andrei dug his hand deeper, watching me hold back the pleasure I was feeling with sick amusement in his eyes; he parted my legs with his and crawled up to my face. "Beg me to," he growled. "Beg me to pleasure you, Adrienne."

His breath was warm on my skin, sending a dark wave of desire all over me. He brought his mouth to mine as if he was going to kiss me. "Beg me, Adrienne."

"Fuck you, Andrei," I roared in a tone lace with want. "I fucking hate you."

His eyes darkened as a certain hotness filled the space between us, then he took my mouth, kissing me roughly, as if he was pouring all the hatred he had for me onto my lips. His groans were deep, and I could taste whiskey and cigars on his tongue. I committed the sin of liking the way his tongue curled around mine, I liked the heat evaporating from his mouth, but I held myself back from returning his kiss.

"Kiss me, Adrienne." His command was harsh against my senses, his voice sensual. I would lose it if he spoke that way, with that baritone that made me lose control over my senses.

My self-will crumbled and failed miserably as his tongue started to move, slowly at first, but it roughened in a mere second. This man had more control over my body than I did; everything felt so wrong yet so right.

I let myself moan, I let myself enjoy everything he did to me, from the vibration of his finger buried deep inside me to the dance of his tongue on mine. Tension froze my muscles and my pulse raced, something built in me. "I'm going to come."

"Yeah?" Andrei whispered with a ragged breath. "Come for me, baby. I want your juice all over my finger," he whispered into my ear. "Come for me, Adrienne."

My body responded to his command, and every part of me trembled. My slow, steady moans turned into loud screams; it was hard to tell if his room was soundproof and with his brothers and Maria around, I wasn't sure it was appropriate to scream. But I didn't have a choice, I was no longer in charge of my body. My eyes rolled into the back of my head as spasms flushed through me.

By the time I came to my senses, I found Andrei had uncuffed my hands…and his towel was no longer around his waist. His erection was the damn longest and biggest one I'd ever seen; I didn't even know if it would even fit into me.

He tugged on the chain bodice of my dress. "Take this off."

I didn't argue, I slid the fucking dress off and let it fall to the ground, allowing myself to be completely naked. Andrei's eyes assessed me like I was a painting up for auction. It made me feel very aware, and for the first time, insecure. I should have taken the gym seriously. I cupped my breasts with my hand.

"Kneel."

I complied; he'd turned me into a horny idiot.

"Take your hands off," he demanded. "I want to see everything."

Slowly, I moved my hands away from my breasts and let them fall to my sides. His eyes beamed with something I couldn't quite pinpoint as he stared at me.

"God, baby. You're so fucking beautiful."

Heat rushed to my cheeks, maybe because he just picked up another nickname for me, *baby.* Or because he just called me *beautiful.* Could have been both.

"Lie on your back with your legs apart."

I gasped, my throat dry with a slutty thirst.

"Now!"

I lay on my back, spreading my legs with my eyes closed. I heard Andrei's footsteps and he came to me before I felt his paper-light touch on my thighs. "Beg me to lick you, *malysh.*"

There was no way I'd beg him, he either wanted to or not. But that was until his finger slid into my pussy; this man would make me go insane. "Please."

"Say it like you mean it, baby."

"Lick me, please," I panted. It was hard not to with the way his finger was curling inside me, hitting my g-spot repeatedly.

Another finger slid inside me, and then soft wetness followed, teasingly at first then with a slow vertical rhythm. I twisted my waist, riding his tongue and fingers, thinking of all the possible ways I'd kill him.

"Do you still want me dead, *malysh?*"

Yes, echoed in my head while, "No," came out of my lips. I was conflicted, but maybe I'd be clear-headed after riding his tongue.

He increased his speed, sliding his fingers in and out of me. "You're dripping like the fucking Niagara Falls, baby. So wet."

A second orgasm took over me, stronger this time, and longer. With the way my moans were almost deafening me, it'd be a miracle if everyone in the mansion weren't awakened. Either that or they were dead.

Andrei yanked my feet and tossed me around so that I was on all fours on the bed with my ass raised at him. He spanked my ass and I yelped in pain.

"Do you want to kill me right now, *malysh?*"

I didn't give an answer, and he took his revenge with another spank.

"Answer me."

I held back.

Spank, spank, spank.

My ass felt like I'd been sitting on a pile of lit firewood, tears blurred my vision…and pleasure throbbed in my pussy. Wasn't it weird, how something causing you pain could also bring you pleasure? This pain made me feel afraid, yet also made me feel comfortable.

He thrust into me without warning. I let out a scream and my chest collapsed on the bed. He slid his hand beneath me and grabbed one of my breasts, twirling my nipple so hard it hurt. "Know this, *malysh.* From the moment we met, you became mine." He groaned roughly. "And mine does exactly what I say."

His hand went from my breast to my neck, choking me while his other hand gripped my waist. "And you keep disobeying me."

I couldn't make out the rest of the things he said as they came muffled between my own moans, my pussy clenched around Andrei's dick as my body prepared for a third orgasm. Andrei's thrusts became faster, his grip on my neck tightened, and his groans grew deeper.

After a few more thrusts, our moans collided as we climaxed. Andrei didn't pull out, he held me steady as he filled me with warm semen.

Then he released me and let me fall tiredly on the bed.

"One more thing, *malysh,*" he said, trailing his hands on my ass. "Don't ever try to fucking kill me again."

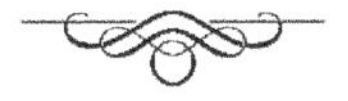

The morning after a good fuck never really felt good. My body started to ache dully as I opened my eyes.

Delicate rays of morning sunlight stalled on the thick white drapes. If the drapes were any darker, it would be hard to tell when it was dark or bright outside.

Heat radiating from Andrei's bare chest warmed my back and I wondered what his temperature was on a normal day—probably up to forty degrees Celsius or even higher. After last night, it felt like things would be different between us, but whether it was good or bad I didn't know yet.

Cowardice had never been one of my characteristics, but I found change was inevitable sometimes, and now, I'd changed into a coward who couldn't turn around to face the man she'd begged to fuck her just last night.

Andrei moved behind me a little and I shut my eyes, pretending I was still asleep. "I know you're awake, *malysh*."

Shit! I was definitely going to kill this man; anger brushed lightly in my chest and gave me the courage to turn around. I was sure my eyes dilated as soon as I turned. He looked like a fucking bad Greek god, and I wasn't even exaggerating.

His curly raven hair was disheveled in a sexy way, his cloudless-blue eyes peered at me with the softness of daisies, and my God, he had to do something about those broad shoulders and toned abs because it would be the freaking death of me. I bit my lip, remembering this sexy ass man kissed me last night. *He fucked me, hard.*

"How was your night?" He smiled in a way that said he was teasing me.

I rolled my eyes. "Could have been better." I still had to preserve whatever self-esteem I had left.

Andrei's smile only widened, showing off his fine set of white teeth. "Could have?"

"Yes," I answered sharply. "For a mafia boss who's probably fucked half the women in New York, your skills at pleasuring a woman suck." It was the biggest lied I'd ever told. Truthfully, I'd be a slave if that's what it would take to have him inside me again. The memory of his tongue on my pussy made my clitoris heavy with a certain craving that only Andrei could satisfy.

"Are you sure about that?" Andrei raised a hand and caressed my cheeks very softly. "You're blushing so much that I'm afraid you'll turn into crimson flames."

I was caught. He must've known how good his sexual skills were that it didn't matter what lie I told him. If only he'd try to make his heart skilled with a little bit of kindness too. "I need to use the bathroom."

I tried to raise my body, but it fell back down and an unexpected pain shot through me. *So much for a good fuck.*

"Are you okay?" I must've been hallucinating because something appeared on Andrei's face and it looked like concern…for me.

"No, I'm obviously not okay." I grimaced. "Thanks to a certain sex animal." My joke disappeared in the air as his face was still drawn together in worry.

"I was too rough." He examined every part of me, from my back to my thighs, then my hands and neck. "I should've been gentler."

My heart melted with his words. Andrei-freaking-Levov, king of the Bratva mafia and notorious crime leader, felt guilt for hurting me. I needed to record this and keep it safe because I was certain the odds of it happening again were very unlikely, just like the odds of my heart melting for him again. "Don't act like that, it's annoying. Plus, I'm tougher than I look."

"Sure you are." His eyes were on my back. I could tell the marks from my papa's whips still disturbed him. I could tell he was curious to know what really happened, but I wasn't ready to tell him, not yet at least. So I asked something I thought would lighten the mood.

"How long have you had your tattoo?"

He removed his gaze from me. "It's been twenty years." He ran a finger on it. "There's a woman I knew, she was an artist."

There's a woman. The notion that he had a permanent souvenir from another woman left an unsettling feeling in my stomach. "Was she your lover?"

A lazy smile played on his lips. I couldn't shake off the feeling that he was probably remembering all the happy memories he had with her, all the times he'd fucked her like he'd fucked me last night. "She was more than a lover."

Venom seeped into my heart. "A wife?" Come to think of it, I found it strange he was not married at forty-two; most men in the mafia married early and produce kids to carry on their sick legacies.

He did not see it fit to answer my question because he muttered, "You're one curious cat, *malysh,*" brushing off my question like it was a mere disturbance.

I wasn't going to back down though. "Why do you have my name on your chest?" I thought of a way to bait him into giving me an answer. "Or is it her name?"

"It was a name dear to her," was all he said before climbing out of bed. "Let Maria know if there's something you need, I have a meeting this morning."

“I want a tattoo.” I wasn’t sure why I blurted that out considering I had never even thought of getting a tattoo before now; my papa said they made women undesirable. “And I need new clothes.”

“As long as you promise to behave.”

I nodded. “I will.”

“Alexei will take you,” he said picking up his towel from the floor. “There’s a card in the lower drawer, it’s limitless.”

“Good, because I’m a good spender.”

“I don’t care how much you spend as long as you stay out of trouble,” was the last thing he said before disappearing into the bathroom.

I had an eerie feeling that Andrei and I were about to become more than enemies. It made me anxious for some reason because one of us needed to die for the other to live.

Chapter 15 - Adrienne

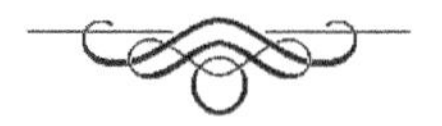

Andrei definitely chose Alexei to chaperone me out of spite, that much I was sure of. The man hadn't moved his eyes away from me since we entered the tattoo shop, but that was less of a problem compared to the fact that he hadn't spoken a single word to me for the past three hours since we left the house, not even when I asked what type of tattoo his brother would like.

Truthfully, I'd only asked because I wanted the exact opposite of what Andrei would like, but when Alexei returned my question with a glare more terrifying than death itself, it made me feel like I was being ridiculous. He was probably one of the old-school kind of guys that thought women had no right to tattoos. Most men in our world were like that, closed-minded and misogynistic. *Ewww!*

"They're so pretty," the tattoo lady said to me with a beam. "How did you think of something so lovely?"

I glared at Alexei standing by the door like a mannequin made for the gym and then gave the tattoo lady my kindest smile. "I got the inspiration from someone…awful."

She let out a loud laugh that tried to conceal her anxiousness as she tried to figure out if I was being serious or sarcastic. "Whoever it is sure has a style."

I scoffed. "His style is not smiling or wearing shoes, you know how the Russians are," I replied, simply to annoy Alexei. I knew how exasperated Russians get at that misconception, though I knew the shoe one was a lie. But I kind of believed the smiling one because the living evidence of it was standing in front of me while the other had fucked me last night.

Which was the reason why I chose a tattoo of thorns and roses with smiling skeleton heads. I wondered how Andrei would react to it.

"That's…weird."

"It is." I got up to my feet. "Thanks for the tattoo."

"You're welcome," she said. I could feel her smile fade as I turned my back on her and left the shop with Alexei behind me.

We got to the car and drove quietly to a clothing shop on the outskirt of the city where we were certain no one would recognize me. I was gone for a while and my papa was probably searching for me by now. We couldn't risk letting him find out where I was.

Alexei pulled over in front of the white giant building that was made up of more glass than concrete. I peered around cautiously before getting down from the car. Alexei meant to come with me, but I leaned on the window, knocking on it and waited for him to wind it down.

"I'm not letting you come inside with me," I said to him. "I don't need a babysitter, especially not one so huge and grumpy."

Alexei stared bullets at me. "I do not take orders from you."

"You don't, and I am not giving an order." I breathed. "Don't you think it would be more suspicious if you followed me inside?"

He didn't look like he thought so.

"You can wait here, to make sure I don't run away."

"I don't care if you do," Alexei said, peering at me through the rearview mirror. "If it will keep my brother safe, I don't mind if you get on your heels right now and never look back. I wouldn't run after you either."

That was the first time I'd heard Alexei say that many words. He mostly always replied with a nod or a simple word but for some reason, he looked pissed at me right now and I couldn't even tell why.

"What is the matter with you?"

"You're an Italian. Dante Paolo's blood," he said matter-of-factly. "I don't trust you not to betray my brother or try to hurt him. I don't know what your mission is but hurt my brother, and you die."

I scoffed. I must've been hearing him wrong. "Dramatic much, Alexei?" Rage made my vision red because how could he dare to act like Andrei was the victim here?

"You seem to be forgetting I am the one who was held at your brother's mansion against my will," I growled. "Do I need to remind you I am the one who was forced into a marriage I didn't want in the first place?" My vision blurred because I was at the edge of crying out my fury. "If you hated and distrusted me so much, why didn't you try to stop your brother from marrying me?"

Alexei rubbed his face frustratedly. "I tried."

"Well, you didn't try well enough, Alexei," I said. "I didn't want any of this. All I wanted was to pay back my father in the same coin he did me all my life. That was the reason I approached Andrei. But being held hostage, getting married, and growing these feelings were never part of the plan."

I was being sentimental, but I didn't care. I couldn't care. "You're his brother, but you sat back and did nothing but only now, you try to make me the villain and Andrei the victim?"

"I'm not making you out to be the villain, Adrienne." His voice was calm and polite now. "I'm only trying to protect my brother?"

"From who? Me?"

"You're Italian, you know exactly what I mean."

I laughed. A sneer meant to mock Alexei's double standards. "And who will protect me if things were to go awry? Who would protect me if I woke up one morning and discovered your brother had been using me all along? Who would protect me if he started to think of me as boring and useless?"

"It won't come to that."

"And if it does?" I asked firmly. "Will you stand up to him and tell him it is wrong?"

Alexei didn't answer.

"I thought so," I concluded. "Everyone in this world is the same. Cunning and selfish and looking out for their own."

It was different for me, though. No one was looking out for me. Sometimes I thought that the reason I got so attached to Andrei was because he cared for me in the way no one else did.

He worried if I got hurt and tried to protect me. My papa was supposed to do all of that for me. He was supposed to love and protect me like other papas did for their little girls. But mine turned me into a dirty killer.

My hands balled into fists as anger shot through my vein. "I've only started to make something good out of my situation," I told him. "I've started to get comfortable with Andrei and I've started to feel at home now. The last thing I need is to feel threatened when I've started to make my own path."

I leaned forward so I was positioned between the driver's seat and passenger's seat. "I will kill you if you try to mess things up for me. I know you love Andrei, but I like him too. Maybe not in the way a wife should like her husband, but I do like him." *A lot.*

We remained silent in the car.

Alexei was probably trying to process everything I'd told him, and I was trying to process my own feelings.

This was the very first time I'd admitted I liked Andrei, but even the pope wouldn't get that confession again from me after now. And I probably wouldn't even admit it to myself after this moment.

Still, that was the truth, and I wouldn't let anyone take away my chance at truly being happy. Not even if it was the brother to the man I'd come to like.

"Be careful," he finally said. "I'll be watching you."

"I'll be watching you as well," I said. "Now are you gonna let me go shopping? And I don't need you to babysit me."

"Andrei would be mad if he finds out I let you go alone."

"You didn't sound like you cared if he was going to be mad minutes ago."

Alexei's frustration was obvious from the way he pinched his brows together. "Go, and you better make it quick."

I opened the car door. "No woman shops that quickly." Especially not a woman who had no clothes of her own.

Walking inside made my breath cut more times than it needed to as anxiety that my papa or one of his men could grab me from behind at any time made my stomach churn. I'd almost forgotten about his numerous cruel punishments in just a matter of days. I detested the possibility of returning to that situation again.

"Good afternoon, ma'am," one of the shopping assistants greeted me as I walked to the women's section. Her blonde hair was tied into a bun, and her brown eyes gave me a polite look. *Sophia* was written on the card that hung around her neck. "How may I be of assistance to you?"

"I need something expensive."

She gave me a full-length glance, condescension lurking being her polite smile. "Uhm…"

"What? You think I can't afford to buy something expensive?" I'd worn another set of Andrei's oversized baggy shorts and tees which I understood could make me look shabby, but they were designer and looked as expensive as they felt on my skin.

"No, ma'am, not at all." She gestured for me to follow her. "I'll show you our new arrivals."

"Thank you," I said, holding a confiscated smile.

I spent the next hour picking out new clothes, bags, and shoes and by the time I was done, my knees were weak and my stomach was rumbling. I regretted not having breakfast before leaving.

"Your bill is fifty thousand dollars, ma'am."

I removed Andrei's credit card from my shorts with glee and handed it to Sophia. It felt good spending someone else's money, at least someone who wasn't my papa, not that he limited how much of his dirty money I spent. I just didn't enjoy spending it as much as I was enjoying spending Andrei's money right now.

Sophia left for a moment, she returned with a receipt and Andrei's card a few minutes later. With a smile that reached her ears, she handed me a receipt and Andrei's card. "Thank you for shopping with us."

I smiled back, not knowing what to say in response.

"If you'd like, we can help you carry the bags to your car."

"I don't think that will be necessary," I said as I rose to my feet. I grabbed the ten shopping bags. New items in nine and the clothes I'd worn into the mall in one of them. I'd tried on a short pink dress with puffy short sleeves that clung to my curves, and a limited edition, black designer slippers heels—I wasn't in the mood to go into the dressing room one more time so I decided to wear the new dress home.

My eyes made contact with a certain diamond pentagon cufflink, glittering behind a show glass as I left the women's section. Andrei wore suits most of the time, and it would be generous to get him a gift—even if the money from that gift came from his own pocket.

I walked inside the jewelry shop and bought a cufflink worth one hundred and sixteen thousand dollars for my archenemy. The thought of a smile on his face as I handed a gift to him sent a tingle through my chest and an unconscious smile to my lips. What were the odds of someone being happy to receive a gift gotten with their own money? I wasn't sure, but he'd have no choice but to accept it with gratitude.

"Adrienne."

I froze as an unfamiliar voice called my name behind me. Adrenaline contacted my blood vessels, sending a mixed signal to my brain and making me confused about what action to take. *Turn around and fight or run?*

Running would make me look like prey, and I wasn't even sure who this person behind me was, so I turned. A gleeful feeling wiped away the previous adrenaline as my gaze fell on Oliver-fucking-Mason, my first love—who wasn't exactly a first love—but my high school crush. Ugh.

"Oliver!" God, he'd always been hot, but right now, he looked like a ball of fire itself. "Jesus Christ." Excitement seeped through me.

"Yeah, Jesus Christ, Adrienne." His black eyes sparkled, just like his wide grin. "You look so hot."

"Do I?" His compliment made my cheeks flush. "It's been like what? Forever?"

"Forever is an understatement, truthfully." He rounded the area what his gaze. "What are you doing here? And what is that you've got there?" He squinted at the diamond cufflink in my hand. "Let me guess, your dad? Your lover?"

"Neither." Andrei was not my lover, yet a slight amount of guilt tugged on my heart. "It's for someone who isn't even a friend."

"I see." Oliver nodded. He brushed his brown hair with his hands. "Do you mind joining me for coffee at the café downstairs?"

Alexei was waiting outside, and I didn't think Andrei would take the matter lightly if he knew I was chatting away with an old friend while keeping his brother waiting. "No, maybe some other time."

My stomach chose to be the villain in my life's story; it rumbled, calling Oliver's attention and mine to it.

"You sure?" Oliver asked, giving me a defeated look. "I think you may need some snacks too."

I heaved a sigh. "Fifteen minutes, that's all I have to spare."

"Works fine for me."

He helped me carry half the bags and we strolled to the café downstairs. Three minutes later we'd gotten our coffee and I had a hamburger to quench my hunger. We chatted about meaningless things; he told me how he'd become CEO of his dad's company and all the other information I could've spent the rest of my life without knowing.

"Tell me, Adrienne." He leaned back on his French bistro chair. "Are you seeing anyone?"

I bit down on a mouthful of burger. "No. I don't think I'm in the situation to date just yet." It was the truth, dating was a sin that came with a lifelong tainting of one's name in our underworld, especially for women.

"Too bad." His countenance changed into a sad one. "I wanted to ask you on a date next time we meet."

Another bite of my burger. "Unfortunately, you can't."

"I think I still have a chance, you can make exceptions," he said confidently.

"Well, I can't." I had a feeling our catching up would turn sour soon. "I think I should go now."

"Come on, Adrienne. Don't try to play hard to get." He leaned forward, sending the urge to stay alert to my brain. "I know you liked me in high school, you'd have done anything to have me as your boyfriend."

This would end badly. "It's a good thing we're no longer in high school then, don't you think so?"

He laughed, a low, insulting kind of laugh that you'd often hear from the bad guys in movies. "I wasn't gonna date you then 'cause you weren't one of the modelish kind of girls. I mean, your breasts and ass were bigger than the other girls. You know, not so hot back then."

Was this motherfucker body shaming me?

"But now, I kinda want to know what it'll feel like to spank that ass and fuck you from behind."

"You'll only get to do that in your imagination. Spanking my ass and fucking me from behind, I mean." My patience was running out. "Thanks for the coffee and burger but I think it's best I leave now."

I picked up my shopping bags and turned to the exit when he grabbed my hands. Disgust grew in my stomach.

"I want to fuck you, Adrienne, just once. Huh?"

Okay, that was it. My patience was exhausted. I turned to him, narrowing my gaze at his balls, before I could raise my legs to kick them, someone flew past me at the speed of light. Before I could register who it was, Oliver was writhing in pain on the floor.

A familiar rosewood perfume filled the air, and a dark aura possessed the environment.

CHAPTER 16 - ANDREI

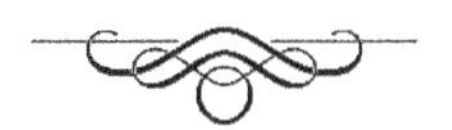

Adrienne Paolo was going to be the death of me—that was a fact I didn't need to deny. Sitting in this dark container with these freaking Chicago Al Capone was the last place I really wanted to be, especially not when I had an ass as soft as Adrienne's to get back to.

It'd been five fucking hours since I left her earlier today, yet I couldn't get the image of her naked body out of my head. Her delicate olive skin, her full breasts that kicked every sexual nerve in me into action, and *Christ,* her loud moans.

I took a pack of cigarettes out of my suit jacket, pinned one between my lips, and lit it. Every pop sent smoke and dirty images of my little slut to my head. I'd even lost control and fucked her so roughly that her skin was purple with marks this morning. It was probably for the best that I marked my territory on things that were mine.

My phone bleeped; it was a message from Alexei. He'd sent a picture of Adrienne's tattoo; she'd made one that looked almost like mine except for the fact that the skeletons on hers were smiling. My *malysh* had a fucking sense of humor, which I needed to set her straight on tonight.

Another bleep came in an hour later. It was a message from the bank telling me she'd spent fifty thousand dollars of my ill-gotten money on clothes. I wondered if she knew she'd have to pay for it. I had to think of a way for her to do that. Having her wrap her smart mouth around my dick and sucking it like her life depended on it probably wasn't a bad start.

The previous bleep was followed by another one, still from the bank, which I ignored. And then another one from Alexei. Adrienne was sitting in a café with a guy, surrounded by shopping bags. Her smile was brighter than I'd ever seen it.

My jaw clenched, and my heartbeat doubled—this feeling was new. It made me want to smash something, to kill someone, and I knew who. I hated that Adrienne was sharing the smile meant for me alone with some other dude.

Me: Send the location.

Alexei: *typing…*

I shot up from the chair and gave the men in the container my meanest stare. "Let's have this meeting some other time, something more important came up." I saw the displeasure in their eyes before I turned my back on them, and I didn't give a flying fuck because they knew better than to try to argue with me.

My car was already out of the driveway when Alexei's text came in. I pulled into the road like I was reenacting Fast and the Furious, at a speed of 120 meters per hour. It was either I drove straight to hell or the fucker sitting with Adrienne went straight to his maker. I knew which option I preferred.

I reached the clothing store less than twenty minutes later and parked beside Alexei. "Where are they?"

He nudged his head in the direction of the café, and I started inside. As soon as I reached the door, Adrienne stood as if she wanted to leave, and the piece of shit held her back by her hands that only I was supposed to touch.

My own speed scared me as I hit the guy, causing him to fall on his back on the ground. He hadn't had the opportunity to react when my hand met his face again, again, and again. Before I could bring myself to stop, his face was already an unrecognizable mess with blood exiting his nose, a busted lip, and a purple, swollen face while my hand was bloody and bruised.

"Stop it, Andrei!" Adrienne's voice came muffled from the background in a plea. The fact that she was begging me to leave this guy who dared to touch her made my pulse race even more. I gave him more punches, leaving him only after he'd passed out.

Adrienne's eyes were wide with shock and her hands were thrown over her mouth when I looked at her.

"Go outside, Adrienne."

She didn't move. Her eyes were still dilated in horror. What did she expect when she was driving me so fucking insane?

"Out, now!"

She flinched at my roar, then picked up her shopping bags and left the café. I tried to steady my breath and calm the storm raging inside of me before joining her outside. I asked Alexei to tidy up the damage I'd done before sliding into my car.

Adrienne's lashes were wet, as if she'd been crying, and I didn't want to console her because I was so fucking mad myself. I ignited the car and drove us home.

Adrienne was the first to leave the car when we reached home. She banged the door so hard they'd probably moved out of place and stormed inside, abandoning the clothes she'd spent my money on. I followed her immediately, calling her name and radiating with anger as she ignored me, went up to her bedroom, and locked the door behind her.

"Open the door," I called from outside, trying to keep my voice as neutral as possible.

She ignored me.

I hit the door. "Don't make me break it down, Adrienne."

"Do your fucking worst, asshole," she yelled from inside.

This woman was driving me beyond my limit. "Don't test my patience, *malysh*." I didn't mean for it to come out as a roar, but it did.

I kept banging on the door for the next few minutes while Adrienne completely ignored me. I moved back and with one kick of my leg, the door flew open. Adrienne was still wearing the dress she came back with, and she looked stunned that I'd actually managed to open the door.

She probably hadn't learned that I didn't bluff.

"What the fuck is wrong with you?"

"I should be asking you the same, Adrienne." Animosity seeped through us both. "Who do you think you are to hurt my friends."

"He wasn't your friend," I yelled. "You're not allowed to have any friends, Adrienne. Not a single friend."

"And who are you to make that decision for me?"

I covered the space between us. "I own you, Adrienne, you better get used to that."

"Own me?" She scoffed. "No one owns me, not even you or my fucking dad. I'm not a piece of furniture or a gun you fuckers use to do your dirty businesses."

"I am not using you." Why was I trying to lighten the mood? She was the one who messed up. The image of him holding her wrists flared my annoyance once again.

"Then what are you doing?" She firmed her gaze on me. "Keeping me here as your sex slave while you keep tattoos and memories of other women safe in your heart?"

"Yes," was all I said, as doing otherwise would only leave me weak and vulnerable, and those words had never been attributed to me, not until Adrienne Paolo.

She shook her head, her gray eyes overcome with a bit of disappointment and sadness. "Fuck you, Andrei. I hate you."

The harshness in her tone stirred the part of me that was a predator. The faster she ran the harder I'd chase. For someone who was the daughter of a bastard like Dante, she should have known better.

I took a step forward and she took a step backward. We continued in that rhythm until her back hit the wall and her palpitations reached my ear. "Repeat what you just said."

She swallowed, panting like the prey who'd just fallen into the predator's trap. "I hate you, Andrei."

I placed my hand on the wall above her, watching every expression and movement that came from her. "I don't like you very much either, Adrienne." I brushed my hands on her lips, and then moved them to her dress. "Take this off."

"No," she breathed.

"No?"

"No!"

"Fine." I placed my two hands on the round neck of the dress and ripped it apart. "Tell me 'no' one more time."

She didn't.

The dress fell to the ground, leaving her in a red lace panty and no bra. I cupped her breast with one hand and trailed down to her clitoris with the other, rubbing it from the outside of her underwear.

Her breath was shaky, as if she wanted me to do more things to her. I stopped and moved away from her. "Touch yourself."

"What?" Her cheeks took on a dark shade of pink.

I smiled devilishly. "I want to see you touch yourself 'til you come." I pointed to the queen-sized bed in her room. "Go to bed."

She shifted from the wall and moved to the bed while I sat on the vanity across from it, watching her. She parted her legs, her pink clitoris staring back at me. "What if—"

"Make yourself come," I cut her off. "Be a dirty little girl and entertain me."

She nodded, cupped one of her breasts in one hand, and slid a finger into her little cunt. *Fuck,* blood flowed to my groin, making my dick hard and craving some of that pussy.

Adrienne's low moan unsilenced the room. *God!* How much I loved watching her pleasure herself. She tensed after a few minutes, her moans louder. Her climax was short and intense. Then she left the bed and came to me, throwing every piece of clothing I had onto the floor.

"This is how to be at my mercy, Adrienne," I whispered to her. "Now be a good girl and fuck daddy hard."

She bit onto her bottom lip with her upper teeth, giving me a dirty look that I'd bet all my coins to see again. She straddled herself on my legs and sat on my dick like it was her throne. I loved the squishy sound her pussy made as my dick filled her. She was dripping with wetness, riding me in a way I knew only Adrienne Paolo would.

I could tell she wasn't experienced, but knowing my dick was buried deep inside her was enough for me; it was enough to make me come. She started riding faster. I knew she was coming a second time and I wanted us to come together so I held her waist to help her ride even faster until she threw her head back, moaning.

I flipped her over on the vanity, taking control of our ride until we both came.

Her head collapsed weakly over my shoulder after she came with my dick still inside her. It became clear to me there and then that I was never going to let this woman go, *ever.*

Chapter 17 - Adrienne

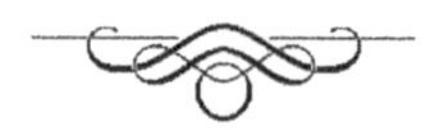

"There's no way I'm wearing that," I said to Isidor, pushing the box of a designer dress in his hand away. "I prefer something more modest."

Isidor squinted at me, probably not believing me.

All my life, my papa had me dressed up in revealing clothes. How else could I attract men to their deaths if I didn't seduce them first?

Remembering it made my tongue bitter and I would really vomit my whole stomach out if I didn't stop trying to replay the memories in my head.

"What do we do? He shopped these for you himself."

Andrei and I had been getting along pretty well for some days now. I no longer got mad when he called me *wife* and he'd been pretty nice to me as well.

He still teased me sometimes though. The man couldn't help his mischievous nature, and I still made out time to taunt him whenever I wanted to as well.

Other than that, we were cool with each other. Almost like a married couple who cared for each other dearly. Who *loved* each other.

Love was out of the equation, but I could agree we cared for each other. We respected each other unless it had to do with sex. We violated each other then.

I was thrilled about Andrei getting me a dress and sending a card asking me out on a date with him. Andrei had never asked me out on a date before.

It was hard to believe he could be romantic in any way, too.

The only time he'd ever done something that his warped way of reasoning considered romantic was when he gifted me Mario's head on our wedding night. I didn't even want to think of how gruesome that was.

"Give it here." I opened my hand and Isidor put the box in it. I placed it on the bed beside another gift box Andrei had sent through Maria just minutes ago.

Isidor's box contained a glittering, strapless, designer dress. I'd opened the other box as soon as it came and it had a pair of black six-inch heels and a tiny black designer purse in it.

"It will look good on you," Isidor said as we both looked at the dress.

I rolled my eyes. "Darling, everything looks good on me."

Amongst all the Levov brothers, Isidor was the closest to my age. He was nice to me and was basically the only one amongst the brothers who could share a smile easily.

Alexei ignored me as much as he could and only talked to me when necessary. I didn't take it personally, as he was that way to everyone who wasn't Andrei.

Dimitri barely came by and when he did, he had this glare in his eyes as if he couldn't wait to dig a hole in my forehead with his gun. *Rude asshole.*

Isidor, on the other hand, was so sweet. He visited me whenever he could and there was never a boring moment with him. He always had a lot to talk about and always cracked the funniest jokes.

I really wondered how someone so loveable was born out of the same womb as the other three mean, cold-hearted mafias. The difference was just too much between them.

Anyway, I was just glad I had Isidor. He was the closest thing to a friend or sibling I'd ever had.

"I know," he smiled, his dark eyes glistening. "You should get ready; Andrei will be here in an hour."

I yawned. I'd been asleep until Maria's knock came on the door. I was still sleepy as fuck, and I really didn't want to go on a date with no makeup considering I probably looked dull. "Do you think Andrei will be mad if we got a makeup artist?"

"You're beautiful, you don't need makeup."

"True," I nodded. "I don't need to, but I want to." I wasn't a 'pick me' girl or whatever people called them these days. I loved looking good whenever I could, and makeup helped elevate my beauty.

And I didn't want to look good because of Andrei. I had no idea why the tiny voices in my head wanted this to be about him because it really wasn't. Really.

"He doesn't like it when just anyone comes in here, Adrienne. No one will hurt him easily, but he'd slaughter the whole city if anyone hurts you."

I gave him a knowing smile because he was trying to tease me. "You're making it sound like Andrei loves me enough to go on a murdering spree if anyone dares to touch me."

I sort of wished he really did. It's sick, *I know*. Who needed a hero who would sacrifice them for the world when they could have a villain who would sacrifice and burn the world for them? Definitely not me.

"The way he looks at you, marrying you, Andrei would never do that if he didn't love you." I chuckled. Isidor was so cute thinking his brother was somehow capable of loving me.

Andrei had grown on me, no doubt, but the only thing he was capable of loving was himself and his brothers. "Don't try to be goofy, we both know he doesn't love me." I carefully placed the dress back in the box. "He hated me even more when he married me."

Isidor shook his head, disagreeing with me. "You're either blind or you're living in denial. I know you can feel it deep down that he does."

"I think I'm blind." I rose from the bed, stretching. "You gotta help me, okay?" I pleaded with a pout.

Isidor was a softie and he fell for it. "Can you do your own makeup?"

"Sure." I mostly always had less than thirty minutes to go on my next hunt after my papa gave me the details. There was certainly no way I would get a makeup artist to doll me up on such short notice.

"I'll get you a pen," he said. "Write down the things you need, and I'll get them."

My pout expanded into a wide smile. "Thank you."

"You owe me one, Adrienne."

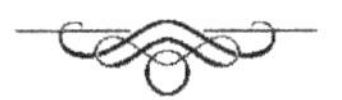

"Do you think buying me a dress will make me like you?" I asked as Andrei opened the door to the backseat for me.

Four other tinted black Mercedes lined up behind us. It reminded me of my papa. He never moved around without security.

The full moonlight and streetlamps illuminated his face in the darkness, and his black eyes sparked with amusement that quickly disintegrated into a blank expression. The soft evening breeze whisked my hair to my face. Andrei reached out to move the hair away and God, the smell of his perfume was intoxicating.

It was a struggle not to throw my arms around his neck and pull him into a tight hug. He looked and smelled too beautiful for his own good.

"Are you getting in or what?" He was clearly not in the mood to be teased.

I furrowed my brows, displeased at his tone. "Are you alright?"

"Yeah. Why?"

"I'm not getting in if you don't ask nicely."

I'd heard this saying several times, *you can't make a wife out of a whore.* But here I was, trying to make a gentleman out of a killer.

Andrei gave me a half-smile. "Please, go in. We have a long drive ahead of us."

I shuddered as I slid into the car. Something wasn't right and I couldn't wrap my head around it. Andrei had sent a card saying we would be going on a date, but the vibe in the air was hot and raw.

This wasn't the mood a couple would have on a date, was it?

There was only one thing I could think of, and my eyes watered as I tilted my head toward Andrei. He had his eyes on the road as if there wasn't a driver navigating the car in the front seat.

"Are you taking me back to my papa?"

Andrei didn't reply, he didn't even bother to look at me, and I had my answer then. "I guess you are," I said quietly.

Panic rose in my chest and my nerves were a wrecking mess. If Andrei was taking me back to Dante Paolo, then I had no choice. I would have to kill my papa tonight and kill myself.

Death was a better fate for me than returning to that hellhole.

"I'd be dead by morning if that's where you're taking me." I smiled, my eyes filled with tears that I didn't even bother to hide. Bold of me to even assume Andrei cared whether I lived or died.

He was being nice to me, and I'd overestimated my importance in his life. I'd forgotten my place. Despite the diamond shining on my ring finger, I was still nothing but a prisoner.

Andrei finally turned his head to me. "You're not going back to Dante Paolo," he said. "I'd be dead before I let you go back there."

"Then what is this?" My stomach fluttered nervously, and my hands were quivering with fear. "Are you selling me off to another one of our enemies?"

"Do you trust me, Adrienne?"

I couldn't believe it. He was calling me by my name, it had to be at a time like this. He was trying to mess with my head.

And it was even crazier because I trusted him. I wasn't going to admit it, but I did. "No, I don't trust you, Andrei. You're still just a man in this dark underworld, and you wouldn't bat an eye before you sold me off if that was what you needed for your dirty business to go on."

Andrei's eyes remained on me for a few minutes. I wasn't certain, but I thought I saw something in them. A glint of hurt. My words hurt him, or maybe I was imagining it.

His fingers fisted around his thighs. There was no way I was imagining that. "If you don't trust me, then there is nothing to talk about."

He looked away from my direction and peered outside the window for the rest of our journey.

The driver pulled over in front of a minimalistic brown building made mostly of glass. It looked like a private suite made for mayors, crime lords, and the like. It was chill.

Apart from a fleet of similar cars parked in the parking lot and the golden chandelier lights pouring out of the glass walls, there was no sign of life here.

One of Andrei's men opened the car door for me while Andrei climbed out through the door at his own side. He tugged the knot on his tie, positioning it in the middle of his white button-up shirt, and then arranged his cufflinks as he walked to me.

"Stay closely behind me, and don't say a word."

"I'm not an idiot, Andrei." I sucked in air. "Tell me what the hell is going on with you. You're scaring me."

He cupped the back of my head and tilted my face so I could look at him. I couldn't read his blank stare. "Don't say a word unless I tell you to."

I should've run when Andrei started to lead the way into the building.

But I didn't. I just went along with him. If he was here to give me up as a sacrificial lamb, then so be it. I wasn't going down alone though.

We entered a checkered floor hallway with an obscene chandelier. The walls were as white as a torture chamber and the silence made my adrenaline pump.

It was really chilly in here, but I kept my back straight, refusing to shiver as I followed Andrei.

The hallway led directly to a white door with men in black lined outside. Andrei nodded to his men and they joined the line, keeping their faces stern and their hands flat on their stomachs. It reminded me of the Ken dolls I used to have as a kid.

Lifeless and immobile.

"Shall we?" Andrei opened the white door in front of us and gestured for me to go in. I hesitated by the door frame, peering at his face for a clue. I needed to know what the outcome of my stepping inside the room would be. Was he going to kill me or let them hurt me?

I wasn't religious, but I said a silent prayer and went in.

The room was dimly lit—but bright enough for me to make out the faces of the men sitting behind a long conference table.

They were all dressed in black suits, and they were all older than Andrei. All eight of them. My stomach was fluttering now; I could throw up.

Andrei took a seat at the head of the table, far away from the edge of the table where I sat beside one of the strange men in the room.

"Is this the girl?" one of them asked. "Dante Paolo's daughter?"

My heart sank into my stomach as soon as I heard my papa's name. I gave Andrei an urgent stare. Was he really here to trade me? Really?

The man beside me drew his eyes all over my body as if I was a bowl of Chinese food and he couldn't wait to devour me. "Italian whores are more beautiful than I thought." He smirked.

"I bet you won't think I'm beautiful when I slice your throat," I spat. I didn't know what Andrei was up to, but I'd had it up to my neck with being insulted by filthy men like this old geezer sitting beside me.

"What did you just say to me, whore?"

"I'll slit your throat. I'm sure you know they don't call me *morte* for no reason."

He flashed a deadly smile at me before he flew to his feet, raising his hand in the air to hit me.

"Touch her and she'll be the last woman you ever touch," Andrei said, his voice as calm as the wind in winter yet as terrifying as a hurricane.

The geezer's hand halted midair. He let it hang for a while, gambling between saving his ego and losing his hand before making the right choice. He retracted his hand, balled his fingers into a fist, and sat back down.

Andrei had great influence over these men; it was evident from the way none of them said a word when he threatened the geezer.

Andrei leaned back in his chair, his face looking every bit the cruel mafia ringleader he was. "No one dare touch her until the deal is finished."

He looked around at all of their faces before pinning his gaze on me. "The highest bidder gets the girl."

Chapter 18 - Andrei

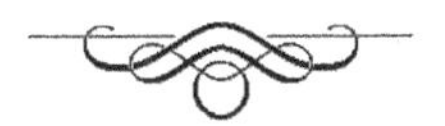

I knew the look on Adrienne's face well enough. She'd never thought I'd betray her. She was hurt and angry.

Her gray eyes had turned pale black and her chest rose and fell heavily with fury when she breathed.

My poor little wife had no fucking idea I'd tear out my limbs one after the other before I let any of the fuckers in this room lay their disgusting fingers on her.

These men were from each of the families here in New York. Someone had ratted me out to them, telling them I had our mutual enemy's daughter in my home.

Honestly, I hadn't even thought of bringing Adrienne to a place like this. I'd planned to take her on a date to the countryside where we could watch the sunrise together tomorrow morning. I had no idea why I wanted to do that, but I just wanted to.

Romance had never been my cup of tea. I usually just fucked and discarded women. I spent my money on them too sometimes, but I'd never even gone as far as buying a flower or shopping for a woman myself.

But it was different with Adrienne. Maybe I was doing this because I'd put her through a lot and I knew she deserved a moment where she could smile genuinely, forgetting the darkness she was born into.

These old farts had asked to negotiate with me on who got Dante's daughter. I wasn't an idiot, I was a businessman, and I could never pass on a good offer.

What they didn't know, though, was that none of them were leaving this place with Adrienne, not even if they offered me the whole of New York.

"I'll give you a whole shipment," the one sitting beside Adrienne said. He'd called my precious *malysh* a whore, and I'd deal with that later because he wasn't leaving here with his tongue in his mouth.

"Three shipments. Surely the bitch can't be worth more than that," another one sitting across from her said.

Adrienne's hands balled into fists. She was shivering with anger, and I'd let her decide what punishment she wanted for that one.

"Five shipments and protection from the FBI," another one chimed in. "I run this city and you know I'm the only one who can protect you from them in the near future.

I scoffed. A near future where I'd need protection from a man like him didn't exist. I had enough powerful allies and although in this dirty business, one could never have enough allies, he made sure he wasn't going to be one when he stared condescendingly at my wife.

"Adrienne darling, come to me," I said. Adrienne was as stubborn as a mule and unpredictable as well; I hoped she would trust me and do as I commanded.

I eased into a smile when she stood and walked to me. As a reward, I put my hand around her waist and lowered her to sit on my lap.

Isidor had told me she insisted on getting dolled up for me, and I hated I couldn't compliment her on how beautiful she was *yet.*

I'd chosen this red dress for her the moment I saw it and I was glad I did. The diamonds on it illuminated her beauty. She glowed in it like a fucking goddess.

I loved how it spelled out her curves and ass. If I weren't so disgusted by the company we had, I'd have been going crazy now with the need to fuck her.

"Seven shipments," I said. "I'm not taking anything less."

The room grew silent and the old farts stared at each other, stalling to see if any of them would take the offer first. "I'll take her for seven," the one who'd been sitting beside her said.

"Place the call now." A deal wasn't a deal until it was sealed and done. I'd learned that from my father.

Men who did the dirty sort of work we did weren't very honest people, and I was one of those men. I even liked to believe I was way worse than they were.

My eyes trailed him as he took his phone out and made a call to one of his underlings, asking for a shipment to be sent to my warehouse.

He peered at me through almost gray lashes when he ended the call. "I've kept my part of the deal. It's your turn now." He propelled his wrinkled hands. "Bring the girl."

Adrienne's eyes were piercing into my soul. Her fear was loud and clear. I raised her hand, the one with our wedding ring on it, and kissed it.

I pulled her close enough to whisper into her ear. "Stay behind me."

She probably hadn't even registered a word I said when I flipped her behind me and flew to my feet, using myself as I human shield to protect her while I slid out a gun from my jacket and started shooting.

The men tried to bring out their own guns, but they weren't fast. I guessed that was one of the curses of getting old. The ones who'd survived my flying bullets laid low on the ground.

I led Adrienne to the table, seeking one of the old farts, the one who'd dared to call my wife a whore and even raised his hand to hit her.

The fucker was trembling when I corked my gun to his head. "Sit up," I commanded.

He did, all while still quivering like the weakling he was. Men like him were nothing before men like me. Men like him lived for intimidating and abusing women and children because they couldn't go one-on-one with other men.

I hated bastards like that.

He sat up, and he'd pissed himself. *Disgusting.*

I kept my gun on the asshole's head and turned to Adrienne. "What do you think I should do with him?" I asked. "Put a bullet through his tongue or chop off his hands?"

Adrienne didn't reply. She huffed, spun around, and walked out of the room.

"Adrienne." Shit.

I knocked the man out with my gun's magazine and ran after Adrienne. She was mad at me, rightfully so. I would be too if I were her.

Dead men lined the hallway. My men had come prepared for this occasion and it didn't seem any of them had been hurt. Alexei nodded at me, asking if they could proceed with disposing of the dead men's bodies and I nodded back.

I couldn't catch a glimpse of Adrienne when I reached downstairs. She wasn't in the car or anywhere around it. I narrowed my eyes at the road, and that was when I saw her.

She was skedaddling down the road as fast as her legs could carry, the diamonds on her dress sparking as the headlights from the cars poured on them.

I opened my car door and slid inside, ignited the engine, and drove after her.

I crossed my car in front of her so that she'd have no place to pass through. "Adrienne," I called out to her as I came down from the car. "Get in the car." I wasn't certain if it was a command or if I was pleading with her. I just needed her in the damn car.

"Go screw yourself, Andrei," she barked. "You must think so little of me. I hate you."

She tried to walk past me, but I grabbed her arm and pulled her back. "It's not what you think, okay?"

Her eyes were crimson with rage. "What was it? You used me as a bargaining chip you cheap asshole."

Most of the passersby had their eyes in our direction. The last thing I needed was for one of them to make a video and bring unnecessary trouble to me right now. I wasn't prepared to take care of Dante Paolo at the moment but if anyone captured Adrienne and me in this moment and uploaded it on the internet, Dante would seek me out.

That was the reason why I had to end those old farts.

"Come with me." I held her wrist. "Let's find somewhere quiet to talk."

She slapped my hand on her wrist, trying to hit it down, but I fastened it even tighter. "What's there to talk about?" she panted. "Are you trying to negotiate me off to the highest bidder again?"

I bit my lips. I wasn't as smart-mouthed as Adrienne and it would be a waste of time trying to argue with her. "No questions. Just come." I managed to drag her to the car after much trouble and drove off.

Adrienne pinned her gaze to the window, watching the streetlights while I drove. We didn't say I word to each other until I pulled up at my vacation beach house one hour later.

"Where is this?" she asked, peering at the small glass house beside the ocean bank.

I undid my seatbelt and hers then got out of the car while she did the same. "This is where I come to clear my head sometimes."

A soft wind blew her hair all over her face and she pushed it aside with a finger. "Why did you bring me here?"

"Because this is where I planned our date," I explained. "I'd wanted to bring you here before I even sent any of those dresses to you."

She snorted. "You think I'm stupid? You want me to believe that?" She stared at me intently, brewing guilt in my chest. "You tried to sell me off like I was nothing, Andrei."

"I didn't try to sell you off. I would never have let anyone touch you the wrong way and you know it."

"I don't," she countered. "I don't fucking know it."

She held her head with both hands and I could see she was struggling to curtail her anger. Her frustration. "I wanted to believe for the first time that I had someone in my corner," she said. "I wanted to believe I had someone to protect me and care for me even if it is a tiny bit."

My heart sank and bled just hearing the sadness edging her voice. "You know I will always protect you from everyone."

She smiled doubtfully at me. "Who will protect me from you?"

"I'll never harm you, Adrienne. You know I'll never do that."

"Why don't I believe you, Andrei?" she said softly. "Why can't I believe a word you say?"

We stood still, looking into each other's eyes. I had no idea what she would see in mine. Maybe she would see I had no soul, or she would realize I had no heart. Maybe she would look straight into my eyes and see nothing more than her captor.

But her eyes were beautiful to me. The scars in her heart were like a treasure I wouldn't give up for the world. I wanted to protect this woman with my life. It wouldn't be enough to save my dark soul, I knew that. But I would be fine knowing I could give her the one thing she wanted.

The one thing she deserved and the thing her mother would have wanted her to have. Someone to care for her and protect her.

"Do you know the last thing your mother told me?"

She shook her head. "No, don't do that. Don't bring up my mother and try to manipulate me into forgiving you because of her. Don't fucking do that."

Adrienne reminded me so much of her mother. The way her gray eyes glistened and the way the edges of her eyes curled whenever she laughed.

Isabella and I were really close. So close that her papa worried we were in love with each other even though we weren't. I loved her, but not the same way I would've loved Adrienne if I could.

With Isabella, it was pure love. I loved her, but I wasn't in love with her.

I'd watched over the years as her papa's obsession grew. He wanted to bite off more than he could chew, and he saw his daughter as the leverage to achieve his greedy goals.

He saw her as a tool, and he used her.

Isabella cried the last time I saw her. She'd begged me to marry her and claim her as mine. I didn't need to do anything else for her but that. She was scared of marrying Dante. She'd been scared of being with someone with the cruel reputation he had, and she was right to have been.

But I'd just become the boss of the Bratva family then and stirring up a fight with the Italians wasn't going to do me any good. Not if I wanted to earn the respect of my family.

So, I'd turned her down, and I'd done it in the cruelest way.

I'd regretted that moment every single day until now. I often wondered if things would've been any different if I took the risk and saved Isabella from Dante. She would have probably been alive, but Adrienne wouldn't have existed.

And Isabella would've wanted Adrienne to exist.

She'd written to me once. A year after she married Dante she'd bragged about being pregnant and having a little girl who would look just like her. She'd expressed her concerns about Dante's obsession with having a son and that was when I should've stormed Paolo Manor and killed that bastard.

I didn't, and Isabella lost her life.

I figured it was only right that I tried to protect the daughter she cherished until her death. I hadn't been able to save Isabella, but I could at least save Adrienne.

"Your mother loved this beach," I started. "She always wanted me to drive her down here so she could see the stars. Aren't they beautiful?"

Adrienne threw her head back and gazed at the stars. She seemed lost in them and she looked so beautiful as the moonlight shone on her face.

Then, as if she remembered who she was and where she was, she withdrew her gaze. "The stars, really?" She crossed her hand over her chest. "You want me to gaze at the stars after you treated me like a can of worms you would easily throw into the ocean to catch fish?"

"I'd cut anyone's throat before they got to treat you like a can of worms."

She pulled her gaze to me. "Is that so? Kill yourself then."

"Would it really make you happy if I did?"

She held back her answer and started to look at the stars again.

"Did my mother ever stand in this spot where I'm standing?"

"Yes," I replied. "She probably stood in every spot here. She loved the way her footprints remained in the sand whenever she walked on it."

"What was she like before my papa?"

I sighed. Isabella was a topic I had never mentioned since she died and that was mainly because no one cared for her story as much as I did. I'd thought to just hold her dearly in my heart forever.

Also, memories of her usually came with great pain. I was left regretting the things I did and wishing I had done things I didn't do when I thought of her. My heart always stung with pain whenever I remembered how I could've saved her.

"Your mother was like a sunflower," I said, thinking back to all the times I'd spent with Isabella. "She was bright, hopeful, and full of happiness. She had dreamy gray eyes just like yours and they would lighten up when she smiled."

"Go on. I want to learn everything I can about her."

"Being born in this dirty world and groomed to be a cruel man, she was the light at the end of my tunnel." I paused. "I hated smiling and I never did it, not after my first kill and not even with my brothers. But whenever I saw her, my lips would twitch, and I would let them curl into a small smile."

"Did you ever think you could have a future with her?" Adrienne asked without looking at me. She was dazed by the twinkling stars in the sky, just like her mother used to be.

"She was kind and pure. It didn't matter that she was born to a greedy underling like your grandfather. She didn't care for our dirty life, and I never wanted to drag her into this mess so I never saw her as anything more than my sunflower."

Adrienne looked at me now. "What if she was a dark and twisted and bloody person like me? Would you have wanted her then?"

I'd never thought of that possibility. I'd never associated Isabella with anything dark. She was a contrast to her daughter. Isabella wouldn't even kill an ant and she was scared of roaches.

And I knew Adrienne's question now wasn't about her mother. She wanted to know if I could think of a future with her. The truth was that I had. Many times, in fact. And I always ended up with one conclusion: I wasn't made for such a commitment.

"No. I'm not certain I would." I didn't want Adrienne to think too much or expect me to love her. I cared for her, and I liked her a lot. But love was something I could never give her. *Never.*

"How was she after she got married to my papa?"

"I never saw her after the wedding," I answered. "Mainly because I was too busy strengthening my reign in my cartel. But when she first heard the news, she started to change."

"Change?" Adrienne pinched her face. "In what way?"

"Her aura completely changed. Isabella never wore clothing if it wasn't very colorful, but that changed quickly. She began to wear dark clothes. That was when she learned how to tattoo, and I was her first client. She changed so much in a couple of weeks. Her innocence faded slowly too, but she was still my sunflower."

Adrienne's eyes sparked in the dark and beads of tears rolled down her face. "I don't even remember her, yet I feel so sorry for her."

My insides crushed just hearing Adrienne say that. "She wouldn't have wanted you to feel sorry for her, she would've wanted you to be strong and tough. And she would've wanted to be remembered for her strength, not her weakness."

"Do you think she would have liked me knowing I am no different from my papa?"

"You're different from him."

"How so? I'm a cold-blooded killer."

"You were forced to be and if she ever found out how much pain you had to go through, her heart would break so much she wouldn't be able to rest in her grave, Adrienne."

Adrienne sobbed silently. She was usually so tough that it felt surreal to hear her sob. And for some reason, her cries pierced my heart like thorns.

"I'm sorry I had to tell you all of this."

She shook her head. "It's okay. I wanted to hear it anyway."

I grabbed her and pulled her close, allowing her to sob into my chest. "Trust me, *malysh.* I will never hurt you on purpose, and I would never let anyone else hurt you either for as long as I'm alive."

"But you hurt me more than anyone else, Andrei," she muttered from my chest. "I don't want to be a bait anymore. I don't want to be *morte* or *slut* used to seduce men to their graves. I want to live my own life now and on my terms. I'll only kill when I want to and only do things I want to."

I nodded, understanding her perfectly. "I know. I shouldn't have done what I did, and you won't ever have to go through something like that again."

"Promise me."

"I promise."

No one would ever get to Adrienne unless they went through me, not even Dante Paolo, and not even me.

I knew Adrienne could take care of herself. She could handle herself in a way that even the men in our world couldn't handle themselves. Still, I wanted to protect her.

I wanted her to feel safe whenever she was with me, and I'd lay the world at her feet if that was what I needed to do to make that happen.

CHAPTER 19 - ADRIENNE

I woke up with my face to the sunrise and the splashing of beach water on the ocean bank. I'd fallen asleep outside on the beach sand last night, leaning on Andrei's chest and listening to his heartbeat while we talked about my mother and watched the stars.

He must've carried me inside because I woke up on the bed this morning inside the glass house, wearing his T-shirt.

After the stunt he pulled, trying to use me as bait, I was certain I would never be able to forgive or trust him.

But something about the way he spoke to me, the sincerity in his voice, and how much he seemed to genuinely care about my mother made my heart flutter.

Andrei was not the monster my papa had made him out to be. He was dark, cruel, and twisted, but definitely not a monster.

His dark eyes brightened whenever he was around his brothers, and they sparkled when he spoke of my mother. *My mother,* it felt so unreal to say.

Before now, I'd never included her whenever I talked or even in my thoughts, but now that Andrei had told me about her—what color she loved to wear, how much she love to smile, and how sunshiny she was—it was really as if I'd known her all along.

I could've even been able to picture her face if I were blind.

I smiled to myself and rolled over to Andrei's part of the bed knowing he would wake up the moment my body hit his. I ended up disappointed because Andrei wasn't beside me. I shot up from the bed, stretched, and ambled out of the room.

Andrei could've been in the kitchen, but it didn't smell like omelets, French toast, or coffee so he definitely wasn't.

The hallway was tinted gold and it was majestic. Andrei had good taste in his interiors. The walls were a sparking mix of gold and white. It looked like heaven here and the view of the beach water outside was serene.

I understood why Andrei would choose to come out here whenever he wanted to clear his head.

It was so quiet that the only thing I could hear was the chirping birds outside and the waves when they slapped the banks.

"Good morning," Andrei said as I stepped into the living area. He was seated on a plain white cushion, his legs propped on a golden granite coffee table at the center of the room. The newspaper in his hands had a strong grip on him.

I sat on the cushion across from him. "Where did you get that?" I hadn't noticed a newspaper in the car yesterday and Andrei wouldn't be reading old news either.

"Alexei delivered it to me this morning."

My chest hummed at the sound of Alexei's name. He always made me anxious for some reason. "Oh, he was here."

Andrei nodded. "Five minutes ago."

"I see." I leaned forward to read the headlines in the newspaper. "What does it say/"

"Nothing. Really," Andrei answered as he closed the newspaper. "Just a couple of things on politics and the upcoming elections. Nothing much about the attack yesterday."

He sounded like he was the one who'd been attacked. "What happened to those men?" I asked. I knew they were probably dead already, but I just needed to keep hearing his voice. It was soothing and I loved to have his attention.

The easiest way to get all of it was talking to him.

"They're in a better place," was all Andrei said. He really needed to learn how to talk more, but I guess we wouldn't be a good match if his mouth moved as much as mine did.

At the very least, he wouldn't have survived this long.

"What do you want for breakfast?" Andrei asked as he tossed the folded newspaper on the coffee table. "I think we should order in."

"I'll take an oatmeal and a large coffee. Oh, and a can of soda, please."

Andrei nodded. He snatched his phone from the couch beside him and made our orders.

"How often do you come here?" I asked, looking around.

An enormous painting of a burning human skull hung on one of the walls while a painting of sunflowers hung at the other end.

Andrei didn't love my mother? *Liar.* He probably didn't even realize it yet. Had it been that he did, they would have probably eloped together. I knew Andrei wouldn't have, though; he'd never leave his brothers behind.

The walls in here were all white. Synthetic green flowerpots stood on every edge of the four corner walls. The furniture was minimalistic, yet beautiful. I'd take lots of pictures in this background if I were one of those social media girls who posted everything.

Sadly, I never had the privilege of using a phone or social media when I was younger, and once I grew to decide if I loved them myself, I'd completely lost interest in them.

Who wouldn't if their lives revolved around deadly mafia men? I wasn't Barbie in her dollhouse. I thought I related more to Maleficent, but even she had a happily ever after loving Aurora.

"I don't keep track of how often I visit here," he answered, looking up from his phone. "But it isn't a lot. I have too many things to take care of to consider hiding away in a vacation house for too long."

"But you have Alexei, he can handle the businesses when you're away."

"Alexei is good, and I trust him the most out of all my brothers to take care of the business when I'm away, but that doesn't mean I still wouldn't prefer to handle my business myself."

"That's fair," I inclined. "How did you take care of your brothers after you became the boss at such a young age? It mustn't have been easy."

"It wasn't," he confirmed. "I was eighteen, Alexei was sixteen, Dimitri was thirteen, and Isidor was only eleven. There were times I wanted to run away and never turn back, but not because I was afraid of being the leader. I wasn't because I'd been prepared for it even after our parents died. I was more afraid of being burdened with the task of caring for three boys."

"Why didn't you run away then?" I teased, knowing full well a man like Andrei would never run away from his responsibilities. He probably had to hear how it was his responsibility to take on the cartel before he could even understand what it meant.

He took my question literally though. "With our parents gone, there was no way I could abandon my brothers. They mean a lot to me, all three of them."

"Yeah." I knew it, and I absolutely couldn't relate since I didn't have any siblings. Andrei got lost in thought. His brows drew together sadly, and his eyes lowered into a dark thing.

I often saw men like him and wondered what they were like on the inside. I knew I hated being born into this world and I couldn't help but wonder if men like Andrei hated it as well.

Would he have wanted something different from this? Could he have had the same dreams that other boys have? Would he abandon this world if he could? Although abandoning this world was impossible. Whatever enemies you made while in it will hunt you down and have your head.

Still, would he want out if he could?

"Are there things you've ever desperately wanted but couldn't have?" I asked. "Did you ever wish to be something different?"

Andrei smiled sadly. "A doctor." He chuckled. "One time when I was five, I hung a stethoscope around my neck and told my father I wanted to be a doctor. I wanted to save lives."

Alright, *now I'm curious.* "What did he say?"

"He took the stethoscope from me and went down on one knee in front of me," Andrei continued. "Guess what he whispered into my ear."

I shrugged my shoulders. "I'm bad at making guesses."

"You can never save lives. You were born to take them."

"What the fuck?" I shuddered. "That's an awful thing to say to a kid."

"It was, but it did help." He brought his legs down from the coffee table. "I never dreamed of being anything else since that day."

Wow! It was hard to imagine Andrei had once been through stuff like that. I had it tough because I was a girl, that was what I always believed. But thinking back, there wasn't much difference between our parents in this world.

They were still patriarchal and deemed women only worthy of being led, fucked, and for breeding. It was the twenty-first century and the world had advanced, but not in our world; women were nothing here.

The men on the other hand were traumatized as kids. Many of them had their first kill between the ages of ten to eighteen. They had to endure all kinds of torture and cruelty at such a young age.

And then they grew, had kids, and did the same to them. It was a never-ending cycle.

"You still haven't told me the things you'd have loved to do if you weren't who you are now."

Andrei sighed, looking reluctant to tell me but knowing he had no choice but to tell me anyway. I wasn't going to leave him alone till I got the answer I needed. And I wasn't asking just to feed my curiosity, I sincerely needed to know.

"A family," he muttered with a strain in his voice. "I think I would've wanted a family of my own. I wonder what it would be like to have a wife and daughters who had her eyes."

"You have a wife." I had no idea why I said that. I just said it. "And you can still have a family. We can have our own little family if you want."

That was possible at least. It didn't matter how we felt for each other. What mattered was how much we respected each other. And I'd come to like Andrei a lot so I wouldn't mind having his children.

"How about you, Adrienne? Have you ever thought of having your own family?"

I shook my head. "I didn't have the time to think or dream of things like that," I said. "I envied other girls who could have such dreams, but I didn't dare dream them myself. I was too busy trying to make up for the son my papa never had."

We both remained quiet, mourning the lives we could never have.

"What happens after you get your revenge?" Andrei asked. "Supposing I let you go, what would you do?"

I smiled at *supposedly I let you go.*

"What would I do?" I asked myself out loud. "The truth is, I don't know much outside our world. Maybe I'd set myself free and fly like the other birds. Maybe I'd just get bored and take my father's throne."

Andrei sat straight. He was clearly intrigued. "You'll become the queen of the Italian mafia?"

"Yes," I agreed with a nod. "Why? Is it so surprising to see a woman rule?"

"Not that," Andrei replied. "You know how misogynistic people in our world are. They'll never let you rule simply because you're a woman."

That was rich coming from a man who forced me to marry him at gunpoint. "Well… are you a feminist yourself?" Andrei may have grown to be nice to me, but I couldn't trust him to see women any differently than the other men. The patriarchy was deeply rooted in their blood and the women in our world enabled it—mostly out of fear or trampled self-esteem.

I was certain I would have too if I weren't filled with rage and the need for revenge.

He squeezed his face. "Feminist is reaching, but I don't think I'd be opposed to a woman becoming a leader as long as she had the balls to take the heat."

"Balls are saggy and useless," I countered. "Look at me, I took the heat and did the dirty work while my papa and his minions took the credit for it. Violence and war aren't the only way to rule, you now know."

"What other ways are there? Violence is the only language they understand."

"Because that is the only language y'all have been speaking for centuries." And even a woman becoming queen wouldn't stop that. But there could be limitations as well. I had no idea why I was even discussing this with Andrei since he probably wouldn't understand anyway.

The doorbell rang and we both looked through the glass walls.

"I'll get it." Andrei pulled his gun out from his back pocket and went for the door. I watched as he opened the door, gave the delivery man some cash from his wallet, and collected our orders.

He walked in with our breakfast and I dived for the plastic bag. There were at least twelve cans of soda in it. "Why did you buy so much?" I asked, taking out a can and opening it.

"You said you wanted soda."

I gulped down the drink and allow the coldness to sizzle down my throat. God, my sugar cravings.

Andrei opened the box while I took out a can of soda for him. I couldn't believe it. I'd despised Andrei so much two months ago. Now, I was digging into breakfast with him.

We almost looked like a normal family. We almost looked like two normal people out to spend some time together. *Almost.*

But we weren't. I made sure to remind myself of that even though I'd seemed to forget it a lot recently. Andrei was my captor, and I had to kill him after I got what I wanted. My heart slowed down just to think of it.

And we'd just passed a hallway of dead men last night. I didn't know how normal people lived but I was certain that wasn't part of it.

A knot tightened in my stomach, and it was hard swallowing the oatmeal in my mouth.

When the day I'd have to kill Andrei finally came, I wasn't certain how I'd do it. I wasn't even sure I could look into his eyes as the life drained from them as I'd wanted to. I wasn't even sure I could do it anymore.

"Still thinking of how to kill me?" he asked, and I fidgeted. "Give it up, you'll never come close to it."

There went his pride. "Beg me and I may make it less painful," I said, willing myself not to let Andrei think I was already wavering. He needed to be on his toes around me. He would be safer that way.

"What do you think Dante's first step will be when he finds out I took you?" he asked.

"My papa is a proud man so being logical wouldn't be his first move." I gave it a brief thought. "He'd gather as many men as he could and attack you."

Andrei nodded. "I guessed right then."

"What would you do if you were in his place?"

Andrei looked at me as if a part of him knew I could betray him with whatever information I was getting from him. He was probably right to.

"I'd do the same," he said. "Like you said, men like us are the same. We have egos too large for our own good. What would you do?"

I choked on my soda and started coughing, hitting my chest. That was unexpected since I've never had to do any thinking. I put the soda can on the table. "I'm not much different either, but I'm calculative. That's how I survived. I'd slowly hit my opponents where it hurts the most, trapping them till they have nowhere to escape to. Then I'd shred them into pieces 'til there's nothing left."

"Smarter than me and the other men."

We ate the rest of our breakfast quietly and tidied the living area before I dragged Andrei outside. He was reluctant but finally gave in since he thought we'd be safer together.

The sun was shiny and bright and the water flowed noiselessly to the shore and back. The sun glinted on the surfaces as the beach water competed with the sky for its blueness. There was a soft breeze, one that carried peace with it.

All my life, I'd never had a better moment than this. A moment where I could watch nature without many worries on my mind. And it was even better because I had Andrei beside me.

Whatever happens between us in the future, I was more than glad he could feel the serenity with me. This once at least.

My hand moved slowly until it hit his, and he opened it, allowing me to hold his. I wished we could have this moment forever. Only then could both of us run away from the rest of the world and away from the dark underworld.

"*Malysh,*" Andrei called my name quietly. I tilted my head to him and our gazes locked. "If there ever comes a day where you'd have to kill me, don't hold back. I won't hold back either."

He tucked a lock of hair away from my face and cupped my chin. "Aim for my heart and never look back."

"I won't," I said. "I'll make sure to hit you right where it hurts the most." And I had a feeling I would break afterward, but I had no idea why.

He smiled at me and his eyes sparkled in the sunlight. "Good girl." He leaned in and our lips brushed each other's slightly before his consumed mine. He kissed me softly, passionately, and I wrapped my hands around his neck.

Even now, my heart was breaking and my peace was replaced with sadness.

I liked Andrei, perhaps too much to ever let him get hurt or even hurt him myself.

CHAPTER 20 - ANDREI

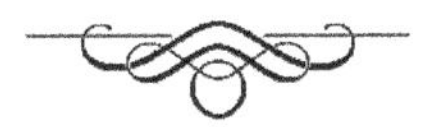

Adrienne did not belong in this darkness with me. I could see it no matter how well she hid it. She wasn't like Dante or me.

She was like Isabella.

She loved the sunshine and the view of the water. Her eyes squinted when she smiled, and she longed for an escape from this world even more than she thought.

And I was going to give her that. I wanted her to be happy and it didn't matter if it meant I needed to give her up.

We'd left the beach house an hour after I received Alexei's call. Apparently, Carlos Amigo, the son of one of the old farts I'd killed, trailed his way to my warehouse this morning and he'd demanded answers on his father's disappearance.

Carlos Amigo was the head of the Mexican drug lords. Fucker had overthrown his father because he'd thought he was too old for the business, and he wasn't entirely wrong.

I wasn't sure what Carlos's relationship with his father was, but I hoped we could negotiate sweetly and easily. If that wasn't an option, I'd regret how much I had to use my gun. I never got involved in a war unless it was necessary.

Some of my men had families and as much as they'd sworn their lives to me, I tried not to waste those lives when there were other ways I could go about it.

"What if they come for you?" Adrienne asked from the passenger seat. She looked anxious. "What if they come for us, Andrei?"

I put my upper lips in between my teeth. "No one will harm you, *malysh.* For all anyone knows, you're my prisoner."

"We're married."

"I forced you into marrying me, remember?"

"You're not allowed to ever die, Andrei. I'm the only one who can kill you and I mean it," she said. "I'll kill you if you ever die."

Her threat pulled a small smile to my lips. Adrienne worrying about me was the cutest thing ever. I barely thought any woman was cute, but Adrienne was to me.

"Don't worry, I won't die easily," I assured her. "You'll have your chance to slice my neck open."

She rolled her eyes. "Good."

I couldn't remember much of what happened next, but I'd been distracted watching Adrienne's face when a car collided with ours, hitting Adrienne's side of the door with so much force that our car tumbled over. The tires screeched in the air and the windows shattered, sending sharp glasses in the air.

The last thing I remembered was Adrienne's bloody face.

Chapter 21 - Adrienne

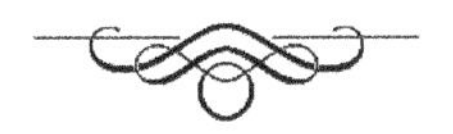

I could hear whistles, distant hums, and muffled voices. The smell of cigarettes and diesel filled the air and there was soreness all over my body that made it hard for me to move.

The last memory I had was sitting in the car with Andrei and I didn't recall anything else happening after that. What happened and where was I now?

My hands were tied and I felt warm liquid drip down my face. I opened my eyes slowly. There was darkness all around me, but it was bright enough for me to make out the feet walking toward me.

Two large feet in what looked like a pair of black cowboy boots edged toward me slowly and calculatedly. I managed to raise my head, blinking up at his silhouette in front of me. He was wearing a cowboy hat and I quickly thought of the Mexican Andrei had told me about.

I couldn't recall his name; I guess I was in really bad shape.

"Look who's awake," he said as he grabbed a chair from the side, moved it in front of me, and sat on it. "*Hola, muchacha!*" He gave me an awkward smile that made me shudder and I saw the gold tooth in his front teeth.

"Who the hell are you?" I mumbled weakly.

"Oh, *muchaha.* Forgive my bad manners," he apologized putting his hand on his chest. "I am Carlos Amigo. I believe you met my father a night ago."

My insides twisted with nerves. "Your father?"

Carlos rolled his head dramatically. "Don't give me that face, *muchacha.* Don't pretend you didn't know my old man."

"I didn't," I said despite the tremble in my heart. "But even if I did, I can't guarantee anything would've been different."

He pulled off his cowboy hat. "That hurts my feelings, *amiga.*"

And then I remembered Andrei. "Where is he?"

Carlos put on his hat. "The Russian?" He shook his head. "I cannot tell you unless you answer my questions truthfully."

"Fuck you and fuck your questions," I yelled. My breath hitched as panic climbed up my spine. "I'll kill you if you touch even a strand of hair on his head. The Russian is mine."

"You don't understand this sweetie, do you?" His wicked laughter resounded in whatever the fuck we were in. It looked like a warehouse of some sort, but I wasn't sure.

He grabbed my chin painfully and revealed a small dagger. "Let's try again, *muchacha,* shall we?"

The feel of his rough hand disgusted me, and I wanted to spit on his face. But I needed to be logical and play along while I thought of an escape. I nodded. "Go ahead, ask your questions."

"Good girl." He patted my cheek and took his disgusting hand away from my face. "Now, where is my father?"

My shoulders throbbed with pain. Fuck. I wanted to get the hell out of here. And with Andrei. "I don't know which of them was your father, a description would help."

"Short, round, and probably wouldn't have been able to take his eyes off you." He stared at my thighs. I was still in Andrei's shirt and goosebumps erupted on my skin from his stare. I would've thrown up if his gaze lingered on me for a moment longer. "My father has a habit of calling women whores."

"Oh." The one who Andrei wanted to shoot off his tongue. Now that I knew he was this animal's father, I wished I could go back in time and cut off his tongue for good. I wondered if he was dead now. "Your father is still alive, but I can only tell you what I know after I see Andrei."

"You're not in the position to negotiate."

"I think I am. You love your father and I want the Russian."

"Fine." Carlos stood from his chair. "I'll send you something to make you talk, maybe his finger."

"You'll never find your father if even a hair on his head goes missing."

"Is that a threat, *muchacha*?"

I forced a smile onto my face. "No. It's only a warning."

"The only reason I'm letting you off is because I do not want problems with the Italians." He walked to me and pulled my hair. "Don't push me."

Shit, *my head hurts.* I endured the pain, not letting him see how much he was hurting me. "I wouldn't dare."

He sighed frustratedly, obviously annoyed by me but not having any reason to hurt me. Or maybe he wanted to hurt me but didn't want to incur my papa's wrath. If so, he shouldn't have tried to cross to Andrei—he wouldn't live till dawn if he did.

The poor idiot probably didn't know how scary the Russians were. Even my papa, as horrible as he was, knew better than to make a move against them unless it was necessary. I guess trying to find his father was, but I didn't think it was worth it considering his papa was an asshole.

"Keep an eye on her," Carlos said and walked out, leaving me with three of his men.

I peered around. My eyes had adjusted in the darkness so I could see better. There wasn't a glass or a bottle or anything useful that I could use around me. I needed to leave here, and I needed to find Andrei before Carlos did something to him.

Seeing where I ended up, I suspected we'd been in an accident and I could only imagine how Andrei looked if I was this messed up myself. I needed to pull a stunt to get myself out of here and there was only one I could think of. I'd used it once, but not in a situation like this.

I'd used it to distract guards at a party organized by one of the cartels in New York. "I need to use the bathroom," I yelled out to the room at large.

The guys ignored me, holding their guns steadily. *Fuckers.*

"Can you hear me?" I screamed. "I need to pee, losers."

One of them turned to me. "Piss yourself, whore." He started to laugh, and the other guys laughed with him. I was going to kill him first.

"I'm on my period," I lied. "You wouldn't want my blood all over the floor, would you?" Speaking of periods, I was certain I was late, but I couldn't think of that right now. "You don't need to untie me, just take me to the bathroom, goddammit!"

"You're so fucking noisy," one of them inclined and finally started towards me. "I can't bear to hear your whiny little voice, it's annoying." He untied the rope binding my body to the chair, leaving only the ones on my hands.

I did a quick mental calculation. My body was throbbing with pain and I was weak but I guessed that I could pull a fast one on them. All three of them were holding guns, but I needed just one to take them out.

The guy untied me and dragged me up from the chair. I hit his stomach with my elbow, put my tied hands around his neck, and moved to the back. The other guys opened fire and I used him as a human shield to protect myself from the bullets.

Fuck. Fuck. Fuck. There was nothing here to hide behind and a human body could only do so much at keeping the bullets away. I grabbed his gun from his shoulder and started firing back. *Two down, one more to go.*

The firing continued till the last guy was down. I rummaged through their clothes, took a loaded .45 and a dagger, and stormed out. I followed a glint of light outside. There were a lot more of them around a campfire, ten at the very least, and they were all armed. I had no chance of taking them down myself. My best bet was sneaking around them, but I'd still be taken down.

I returned to one of the dead guys inside, took their phones, and dialed Alexei's number. "Alexei," I whispered into the phone immediately after he answered.

"Adrienne?" He sounded anxious, as if he'd been waiting to hear from us. He and the rest of Andrei's guys must've been looking for us.

"Yes, it's me."

"Where are you?" he asked. "Where's Andrei?"

"I don't know where Andrei is right now, but I'll find him. I'll send you a location."

"No, Adrienne. Stay put where you are, and we'll come get you."

A sharp pain made my shoulder pulsate. I'd been hit and I had no idea. It wouldn't be long before I lost more blood and passed out. I quickly sent the address to Alexei while still on the phone. "I have to find Andrei. It's Carlos and he seemed like a real psycho; he may hurt him."

"Adrienne no…"

Alexei's protest was cut short when someone pressed cold metal to my temple. "Put the phone down or I'll blow your fucking brains out."

CHAPTER 22 - ANDREI

"Where is Adrienne?"

Carlos laughed, his golden teeth glittering. After the car crash—which the son of a bitch planned, by the way—some of his men attacked us.

Adrienne was passed out and I was still in pain from hitting my head and greatly outnumbered. He'd put a gun to Adrienne's head and threatened to kill her if I tried to resist. I had no choice but to give up and go along with him.

I'd felt so helpless watching them take Adrienne and allowing this idiot to handcuff me to this pole in his office. I was certain hundreds of girls had grinded their bare asses on it for his sick entertainment.

"Where the hell is Adrienne?"

"Easy, *mi amigo,*" he said sardonically. "We don't want your handsome face all wrinkled now, do we?" He trailed his finger on my face and I decided that would be the first part of him I'd separate from his body once I got out of here. If I got out of here.

Last night, we'd killed the heads of most of the crime families in New York, not just the Mexicans, so it would take a while before Alexei and the boys figured out where we were and, knowing this lunatic, there was no way he would let me get out of here alive or keep me long enough to survive this shit.

But I couldn't bear the thought that Adrienne would be caught up in all of this.

"The Italian bitch is a feisty one, I give her that," he announced proudly. "I'd like to see how she'd squirm and try to fight me off while I touch her."

Hot, boiling blood rushed through my veins and I saw red. Crimson bloody red. "I don't care if I die here, but you won't survive it if you touch a hair on her body."

Carlos's eyes widened, then he furrowed his face in a maniac way. "Do you both share a soul?" He bit his finger. "I mean, she said the same thing to me. Isn't that funny."

"It won't be funny when I bury my bullet in your head."

Carlos waved my threat off dramatically. "It would. I'd like to see which of you gets to me first."

"I think that would be me."

Adrienne stood behind Carlos with a gun pointed at him. She had both fresh and dried blood smeared all over her. It was so much that my white shirt on her was soaked with blood. Sweat beaded on her forehead and her skin was pale.

Carlos clapped, his eyes wide with amusement as he burst into laughter. The guy was really a psychopath and that ugly cowboy hat sitting on his head wasn't doing him any good. "Can you see that?" He turned to look at Adrienne and then at me. "Now I see why my father was obsessed with Italian bitches. They have some nerve."

I couldn't mind the fucker now, Adrienne was trembling, and she couldn't hide it much longer. She'd been in pretty bad shape after the accident so I was surprised she could even walk or do anything.

"Put down your weapon, Carlos," she warned. "And move away from him."

"Or what? You'll shoot me?" Carlos broke into another episode of his maniac laughter. "Now I see why they call you *morte.* You're a murderous Italian bitch and you turn me on."

"Too bad sex isn't an option when you're six feet under," Adrienne told him. "Now put your gun down."

"Okay, I'm tired of this game now." He pulled out a dagger from his blazer and started slowly towards Adrienne, slashing it in the air. "You can't shoot me even if you're dying to."

"Try me."

"You would have shot me dead if you wanted to, but I bet you can't," he said. "My men are outside, and they'll come running the moment you shoot, you won't make it out of here alive."

He covered the distance between him and Adrienne and pulled the gun from her and let it fall to the ground. She was barely standing now and struggled to keep her eyes open.

Gunshots started outside and I could hear shouts. Carlos turned to me, his eyes wide with confusion. He started scurrying towards me but dropped dead on the floor in an instant. Adrienne had managed to get the gun and shoot him; my girl took out this bastard despite her weak state.

"I said only I could kill him," she said weakly. "Only I can torment him."

"*Brat!*" Alexei ran inside and started searching Carlos's pockets.

"How did you find us?"

He found the key and unlocked the cuffs. "Adrienne called me. She sent your location to me. Are you okay?"

I nodded. "But she isn't." I ran to Adrienne. She was unconscious now and seemed to have lost a lot of blood. I picked her up and ran for the daylight with Alexei covering me.

"You can't die on me, *malysh,*" I pleaded. "You can't die."

***

Adrienne had been unconscious for two days now. She'd lost a lot of blood and ran a pretty bad fever for two nights. I'd felt some relief when the doctor assured me she would regain consciousness soon, but she still hadn't.

And I hadn't left her side either.

"She protected you," Alexei said. "What will you do with her now?"

In the past two days, I'd come to the conclusion that I'd really hate myself if Adrienne's life was threatened because of me. I wouldn't be able to live with myself and I'd decided to let her go.

I was going to give her a lot of money when she recovered and a new passport. She could settle down in some country far away and start a new life. I hated I wouldn't be part of that life, but I would rather miss her than lose her.

This woman meant a lot more to me than I thought. This woman was my whole life now and I couldn't bear for something like this to happen again.

Adrienne woke up an hour later for the first time in two days. She squinted around. "Andrei."

I held her hand. "I'm here," I said happily. "I'm right beside you, baby."

"Where are we?"

"We're safe and fine." I brushed her hair with my hand. "You were so brave, *malysh*. You saved us."

"Carlos?"

"He's dead. You got him good, love."

She smiled feebly. "It had been so long since I used a gun, I thought I'd flopped and missed him."

I grinned boyishly. I'd not grinned or shown any facial expression at all after I became the leader of the Bratva until I met Adrienne. "You didn't. You did good."

She tried to raise herself from the bed but winced in pain. "Fuck."

I helped her sit up. "Is there something you'd like to eat? Anything and I'll get it for you."

She shook her head. "I don't want food now, I just want you."

I sat on the edge of the bed, took her hand, and kissed it. "I almost thought I'd lost you for good, Adrienne. I was so afraid of losing you."

"I was afraid of losing you too."

I kissed her hand again. "I know, but this won't do. You have to leave."

She narrowed her eyes at me. "What?"

"It's not safe for you beside me," I explained. "I can't go on living if you're dead. I need you to go to a country where no one can recognize you. Start afresh."

"Andrei…"

"No," I cut her off. "Don't ask to stay, please. I'll never forgive myself if you get hurt again because of me. I won't let you stay."

She shook her head. "You're selfish, you know that. How the hell am I supposed to live somewhere not knowing if you're alive or in trouble or dead? Do you think I'd live without you? No, I'd die too."

Her voice was cracking. "Please, Andrei. Let me live beside you like this. Please." She mopped the corner of her eyes. "Dead or alive, I want to be beside you. I haven't been able to make many decisions for myself. Don't take this one away from me or I'll really kill you."

I snorted. She really had a smart mouth, didn't she? She was weak and wounded, begging to stay by my side yet threatening to kill me. I couldn't turn her down.

"Fine, you can stay."

She smiled. A full smile that made her eyes glint.

I held her and pulled her in for a hug. It was my turn to protect her, and I would do it for the rest of my life.

CHAPTER 23 - ADRIENNE

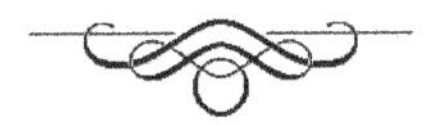

It'd been exactly five weeks and three days since I became Andrei's prisoner and wife. I was starting to feel like this was now my home.

For the first time, someone wanted me as much as I wanted him. It may have been only for sex but then we started to like each other. Maybe I had more than a likeness for Andrei, but he probably didn't feel the same way.

He only liked me, and I didn't mind anyway, it was my best bet at happiness compared to living with my papa.

Andrei had been out of town for a week now, and I had to admit it, even with Isidor who came around sometimes and Maria to talk with—although I suspected she couldn't make more than one sentence in a conversation—the house still felt empty without Andrei's dark aura to spice things up.

And I'd missed fucking him.

Sometimes I forgot he wasn't there, and I looked around to see him. I missed how his grumpy face usually eased into a smile whenever his gaze locked with mine. I'd slowly gotten addicted to his presence without even realizing it.

I slid out of my bed and padded down the hallway to the kitchen. I'd been getting so fucking hungry recently, perhaps it was the boredom from staying indoors all day.

I smelled pasta as I walked into the kitchen, where Maria was cooking with her usual furrowing of brows. She hated me for what my papa did to her family, alright, but there was no way I'd want to remain on bad terms with someone who made most of my meals. "What are you making?" I asked with a smile.

She glanced at me like I was some kind of unwanted guest and returned her gaze to the pot. "Pasta."

"It smells good," I complimented before walking to the fridge to grab a can of soda. "Can we talk?"

She glanced up at me. "Whatever for?"

I took a seat by the island. "My papa," I started. "I know there's no way you can forgive him for the pain he's caused, and I'm not going to ask you to."

She leaned on the other side of the island. "Then what?" Animosity edged in her feminine Russian accent.

"I'm going to help you seek your revenge, that I promise."

"And how are you going to do that?" she asked doubtfully.

I bit back my lips and chose to be honest with her. "I don't know yet, but I'll find a way."

Something that appeared like a smile moved Maria's face just a tiny bit, but it didn't feel genuine. "I know a way," she said.

"Do you?" I opened the can of soda and drank to quench my sugar cravings. "Pray tell."

She placed a full raw chicken on a wooden cutter and took a butcher knife from the set of knives on the counter. "Die." She buried the knife in the chicken, her gaze steady on me. She looked like she was crazy. "Die." She unburied the knife from the chicken and then stabbed it again.

"I-I don't understand that."

"Don't you?" She rubbed her bloody hands on her white apron. "Your papa took everyone I cared about away from me. If you want to help me, all you have to do is die."

I fidgeted on my stool. Okay, this whole conversation was getting awkward.

"Don't you see?" she asked. "The only way to make him feel pain is to inflict the same pain he caused others on him."

Laughter itched the back of my throat at how wrong she was to assume my papa would feel the slightest pain if I somehow ended up dead. The most he'd do would be to start a bloodbath, not to avenge me, but for the sake of his own ego.

For some reason, I felt it would be useless explaining that to Maria since she'd made up her mind that I need to die for my papa to feel pain. There was no way I'd be comfortable eating her food now, not with the way she was thinking. I hated that Andrei wasn't here at a time like this.

I quietly emptied the remaining soda down my throat, threw the can into the trashcan, and was about to leave the kitchen when Camilla walked in, as if I hadn't had enough weirdness for one day already.

"You're still here," Camilla said, rolling her eyes in disgust as soon as she saw me.

It wasn't my job to deal with the other women in Andrei's life—or maybe I was the other woman—so I tried to pass Camilla and leave but she intentionally moved to stand in my way.

"Still being Andrei's whore?" she asked. "I heard he's been out of town for a week, don't you think maybe he is tired of you?"

I'd always been disgusted by women who chose classlessness over dignity, like Camilla, for example. I pondered on whether or not she knew how embarrassing her attitude was. I let my eyes scrutinize her. She was wearing a green tank top with a V-cut on the cleavage area, jean shorts that barely covered her ass, and a green pair of designer sneakers. Truthfully, she wasn't looking bad—I wished I could say the same for her attitude.

"Move out of my way, Camilla. I'm not in the mood for this." Then I wondered if she was the woman who drew Andrei's tattoo. Did he tell her he's not been in for a week? "By the way, do you stalk Andrei? How did you know he's out of town and how long he's been away?"

"I told her," Maria said indifferently. "Do you have a problem with that?"

I suddenly felt like I was in a place where I was unwanted, between my own enemies. "Maybe you should have asked if I had a problem with it before you told her."

"But she didn't," Camilla chimed in. "You must be forgetting you're nothing but a prisoner here."

I smiled. "Am I?" Unpleasantness ran through my veins. "I bet Andrei would disagree since I have his ring." I waved my finger for her to see.

"He's fucking you now just for the feel of it and I know you're aware he married you just to get to your asshole of a father," Camilla spat bitterly. "He'll get tired of it. He eventually does. And considering you're his enemy's daughter, you might just end up in a shallow grave somewhere around here when he is done with you."

Her words were full of venom, and as much as I pretended they didn't affect me, they were infecting me with uncertainty that soon began to fester. "Then so be it."

"What?"

"I do not see how what Andrei does with me should concern you." I shifted my weight to one leg. "Don't meddle in other people's business or I may really have to cut your tongue off."

"I'd love to see you try." Camilla sneered at me, crossing her arms over her chest and tapping her feet. "What? Don't have the guts to do it now that Andrei isn't here?"

"Maybe I'm just giving you the final chance to move out of my way," I said. Truth is, I wasn't sure Andrei would be pleased with me attacking Camilla, especially if she was the woman he talked about that morning. But lord, the thought that she was the woman who had Andrei's heart made me burn.

"This is not your home…whore, and I'm not moving out of your way." She threw the hair running down her shoulders back. "If you really want to pass, then I'm afraid you'll have to crawl."

From the looks of it, Camilla was really here for trouble, and I was damned if I did and damned if I didn't. "I think you missed one more thing."

She narrowed her fiery gaze at me.

"The part where I push you out of my way." Before Camilla understood what I'd just said, I held her by the wrist and dragged her to the other side of the kitchen, then walked away.

My eyes were pinning, and I felt nauseous. My lungs felt like they were running out of air as well. I resolved to take a stroll by the pool, hoping it would calm my nerves.

I'd barely made it outside when I heard Camilla screaming curses at me. "Fucking whore, I'm gonna beat the shit out of you!" She yelled a lot more curses that I chose to ignore and continues to the pool, hastening my steps so she wouldn't catch up with me.

Some women were straight up crazy, and Andrei's possible love for her aside, I wasn't sure I was in the mental or physical place to put up with any sort of craziness. Not today at the very least.

Alexei had left New York with Andrei, Dimitri, and Isidor had gone out for a game and wouldn't be back before night rolled around. I needed them here now and I was sure they wouldn't hesitate to come deal with their brother's distasteful *woman,* but I didn't even have a phone to call them with.

I hated that I didn't have a phone. I'd have to ask Andrei to get me one the moment he returned to New York. It's possible he had many more characterless women in his life, and I wouldn't want to deal with more of them.

The pool area was as cool as I'd expected it to be. Chilled air touched my skin as I walked behind it and swept a chunk of my hair out of my face. How come I hadn't thought of coming here before?

"Wench!" I heard Camilla's voice before I knew she was behind me. I turned around, my vision doubling and my stomach was churning terribly. *Stupid nausea.*

"Say that again," Camilla roared in front of me. "Say you'll cut off my tongue one more time."

It was useless repeating it because even if I wanted to, I wouldn't be able to make out what was her tongue and what wasn't because the world had doubled in my eyes. I'd also probably throw up at the sight of blood in her mouth.

"Not so brave now, are you?" she asked as she fisted my hair and pulled me to her body. I was dizzy and sick, but I wasn't too weak to let a bitch like her throw me around. I grabbed her own hair.

"Let go of me, bitch!" she roared. "Fucking let me go."

"Why should I?" I kicked her knees and she fell on them to the ground, her grasp on my hair still so tight it made my scalp throb.

Camilla pushed me to the ground, causing our grip on each other to loosen. She climbed on top of me and raised her hand to slap me, but I caught it midway and pushed her off.

"Let's not do this. You won't win against me anyway." My vision was spiraling and I didn't know how long I could keep this up. We both stood from the ground.

"You should've been bound to one of those older fuckers' beds now with their smelly balls in your mouth," she sneered. She looked crazy with her long dark hair covering half her face. "Bitches like you are indeed hard to kill."

My hands formed into angry balls at my side. "It was you who told them?" Why didn't I think of that? Very few people knew I was Andrei's prisoner, and those people were limited to Andrei's brothers, a few of his men, Maria, and Camilla.

Camilla was the most likely to do something so stupid.

"You almost got Andrei killed."

She rolled her eyes. "The only reason he would've died was because he had a dumb bitch like you leeching off him. Refusing to die." She started towards me. "I'm going to do him the favor of killing you."

"Don't."

I don't feel so good!

Camilla wrapped her hand around my neck and started choking the air out of my lungs, pushing me towards the pool.

I was weak, really weak. I managed to grab her hair again and push her away and she fell to the ground.

My eyes threatened to shut on their own and I struggled to keep them open, my legs felt weak, and my stomach aggressive. I clutched my stomach, kicking the air as I ambled away from the pool. Away from her because I could feel my consciousness leaving me.

Soft hands grabbed my waist from behind. I wanted to yell for her to stop but I couldn't. With a force, my body crashed into the water. It felt cold on my skin as it swallowed me. My arms were weak and hard to raise, but I tried to float.

Heaviness pushed me deeper into the water. I could feel her hands on my head, refusing to let me out. My stomach kept churning; my oxygen was running out.

I was dying. I was letting her kill me.

I should fight, I should struggle. I had not ruined my papa or told Andrei the whole truth yet. I couldn't die.

I can't die.

But it was too late.

The last thing I heard was Andrei's voice. I was hallucinating his voice even as I died.

And then I died.

Chapter 24 - Andrei

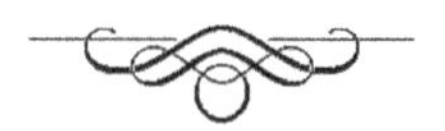

I'd gotten a phone for Adrienne before I scheduled my trip away from New York. I'd wanted to hear her voice every day while I was away and have her tell me everything she was up to.

However, when I thought of her calling bastards like Oliver with the same phone, uneasiness crawled all the way to my chest and sat there, and a certain kind of insecurity sheeted all over me.

I'd ended up keeping the phone. I could give it to her after I returned to New York.

I had no reason to feel insecure since she decided to stay with me of her own free will but Christ, the mere thought of another man even looking at her the wrong way infuriated me.

Plus, I needed to be away from her to sort out this obsession I had with her before it ruined me. No woman had ever been the very bane of my existence the way Adrienne was. I knew she was poison, yet I was willing to drink from her cup again and again. And even if she buried a dagger in my heart, I'd just smile at her and probably fuck her one more time before I died.

I was crazy, truly I was.

I'd thought this trip away from New York would straighten my mind and straighten my thoughts in the way they should be, but it was unfortunate that it didn't. Instead, it had the opposite effect on me. It made me think about her even more.

Being away from her made me miss her little nags and the whines that I hated so much.

I was fucked up, and I knew it.

The door to my suite opened, distracting me from my thoughts. A lady in lingerie walked in with a mask and a whip. I'd always had women keep me company whenever I wasn't busy with my business meeting outside the suite—maybe it was just what I need to get my thinking straight.

She danced in front of me like a dirty feline, making me think of the crazy dirty girl I had at home with the temper of a cat. She kept her ass on my legs, twirling her waist, yet all I could think of was Adrienne's fleshy and curvy ass. Having this woman sitting in the same place where I wanted Adrienne to sit when I got home sent a rush of disgust to my throat.

And the fact that it wasn't just Adrienne's body I was longing for,

It was her voice. The way her presence felt like home to me. The way she never let me get away with anything but still had her way around making me feel she cared for me.

I missed everything about her. And I was longing for her, not just sex with her.

Without warning, I shifted my legs and the woman fell, her ass hitting the floor. I couldn't make out her face but the glitter in her eyes showed she felt embarrassed. A gentleman would have apologized, but I was no gentleman. Instead of making her feel less ashamed about the situation, I straightened my tie and said, "Get out."

Batting her artificial lashes was the only reaction she made. "I should—"

"I won't repeat myself," I cut her off.

She nodded, stood from the floor, and took a walk of shame out of my room.

I'd thought my obsession with Adrienne was because of her body but it didn't seem like it now. No. I was certain it really wasn't that.

I missed how beautiful her morning face usually was, especially when the drapes were up and sunlight filtered into the room.

I missed how my heart fluttered whenever she smiled and how comfortable I felt whenever she was close to me.

I missed my wife.

I took my phone from my pocket and dialed Alexei's number.

"*Brat!* Is there a problem?"

"Pack your bags, we're going back to New York." I hung up before Alexei could protest, not that he would anyway.

We landed in New York eleven hours later, and the whole one-hour forty-minute drive to the house was passed with me struggling to conceal my excitement.

"You're smiling," Alexei pointed out one time.

"I'm not," I lied.

"Are you in love with the Italian?"

The question took me by surprise because Alexei was never the type to be direct about his assumptions. Dimitri and Isidor would have, but not him. If he could ask, that meant he'd already made the conclusion that I was, and that was a big problem. Nevertheless, the bigger problem was that he'd used the word *love.* He should've known better than anyone else that such a catastrophic word was not something I wanted to be associated with.

"Love." I scoffed at the insult. "Do you have a death wish, Alexei?"

"It looks more like you have the death wish," he returned. "You can't fall in love with a fucking Italian. Dante Paolo's daughter especially."

"Shut the fuck up, Alexei. I don't love her,"

"I'm sure you don't," he inclined. "Reason why we're going back to New York four days earlier than we should?"

"You motherfucker," I spat at my brother. Half of what he said was true. I was returning to New York earlier because of Adrienne, but that wasn't because I loved her—I hated the sound of that word.

We pulled over at the manor minutes later and I headed straight to my room to look for Adrienne, and then to hers when I couldn't find her in mine. She wasn't there either. I went down to the kitchen to look for her.

Maria jumped back as soon as she saw me, clearly startled by my presence. "Boss, I-I didn't know you'd be back today."

"Well, I am back today." I peered around the kitchen. "Have you seen Adrienne?"

She shook her head nervously. "Not since yesterday."

A part of me doubted her, but I nodded anyway. I could deal with her later, but for now, I needed to find Adrienne.

"Die, bitch. Fucking die." I recognized the voice instantly. It was Camilla's. My heart switched places with my stomach at the thought that it was Adrienne she was telling to die. My legs moved to the pool area faster than they'd ever been. Camilla was standing at the edge of the pool, her hands inside it, as if she was trying to pull something out…or trying to keep someone in.

I didn't have time to think before I dived into the water still with my suit on. Adrienne was not struggling beneath the water which made me think she had been under for a longer time. I carried her out of the water and put my head on her chest to check if she was breathing, which thankfully, she was. I put my mouth over hers and blew air into her, then I pulled away, doing the thirty chest compressions.

Adrienne started coughing up water before I could do a second round of mouth-to-mouth on her. "Andrei," she whispered as soon as she opened her eyes.

"I'm here, baby." She was shivering from the cold water, so I scooped her up from the ground and wrapped my arms around her. "I'm so sorry I left you all alone." A mixture of fear and relief fought over me; fear that I would have lost Adrienne, and relief that she was okay. I truly had no idea what I'd have done if she died. I couldn't imagine a world without her diva aura.

"What happened?" I hadn't even noticed Alexei's presence till he spoke. "Camilla!" he growled.

I tilted my head to Camilla, who looked like she'd frozen inside a fucking pile of snow in winter, and I was damn about to make sure I defrost her. I sat Adrienne up gently; she almost fell over to the side, but I caught her. I wondered how sick she really was to be weak enough for Camilla to try and kill.

"Let me." Alexei put his hand on Adrienne's back to support her. I nodded at him and left her.

"How dare you lay a finger on her?" My roar filled the air; it was enough to make Camilla flinch.

She crawled backward as I edged toward her. I was certain my eyes were the color of liquid fire because it had her completely terrified of what would come next, as she should be. "It was a mistake, I didn't mean to, I swear." She started bawling. I hated her fake tears, so rather than move me, they made me more aggravated.

"Didn't I tell you I'd take your tongue if you dare insulted her again?"

She nodded. "You did—it was a mistake; I didn't mean to."

I nodded. "I know." Then I opened my arms. "Come here." Animosity seeped through the calmness of my voice.

Camilla hesitated, but seeing as she had no choice, she came to me. I placed her head on my chest, running my finger through her hair. "I know it was a mistake, Camilla," I said into her ears. "That is why you must forgive me."

She tilted her head up at me with tear-filled eyes. "No, Andrei, you can't."

"I can." I pushed her so she fell with her back into the pool. The pressure of her body hitting the water sent some of it splashing back up. I waited for Camilla to swim up before I squatted at the edge of the pool, placed my hand on her head, and pushed her back inside the water.

"Andrei, stop." Adrienne's voice came like the softest summer breeze behind me. "Let her go, please."

I tilted my head to her. She looked so pale and sick; I hated seeing her so weak. I wondered how she could be pleading for Camilla's life when she'd almost killed her minutes ago. Maybe this is why I found her so attractive because although she grew up in the same dark underworld that I did, she was not vicious like I was.

"Andrei—" Adrienne's eyes shut as she passed out.

CHAPTER 25 - ADRIENNE

"What the hell do you mean by pregnant?" I asked, completely stunned by the new revelation, as if I'd not been having unprotected sex for the past month. I looked to Andrei for a reaction, but he was holding his usual expressionless stare.

"Four weeks pregnant," the doctor specified. "There's a possibility you would have lost your baby if you stayed in the pool any longer."

My heart clenched, both because I'd just found out I was carrying my enemy's child and because I didn't want the baby to be hurt for any reason. I hadn't even met it yet, nor had I even been awake for five minutes since I got to know of its existence, yet I somehow felt the need to keep it safe.

My life couldn't be more fucked up than it is right now, thanks to a certain Andrei Levov and myself for not keeping my legs together or even requesting a condom.

"You should get enough rest, also eat a lot of iron-rich foods," he explained. "Your iron levels are really low. It's the primary cause of your fatigue."

I glanced at Andrei again, expecting him to say something, but he sat there instead, peering at both of us like a mute. A million thoughts danced in my head.

Was he angry?

Did he think I intentionally trapped him with a baby?

Will he hate me?

Will he accept this baby?

"Leave us if that is all," he finally spoke, his voice as cold as the pool water I was submerged in two hours ago.

If Andrei hadn't come back, if he hadn't saved me, there's a possibility I would have died with my baby before I even got to know I was pregnant. Fear burst into a million ants and crept all over my spine.

The doctor packed up his equipment and left Andrei's room, leaving me alone with Andrei. My heartbeat drummed in my ears. I tried my best not to show my anxiety about what he would say or think of the situation. Maybe Camilla was right, maybe I should have stayed away from Andrei.

I didn't look up even after I heard the thudding of his feet on the floor as he walked to the bed. His warm hands cupped my cheeks and tilted my face till I was looking straight into his eyes. "How are you feeling, *malysh?"*

I heaved a sigh, exasperated by his question. There were more things to worry about than how I was feeling right now. "I am not sure that is the right question, Andrei."

"What would be the right question then?" he asked, staring straight into my eyes.

"I don't know." I bit my lips, holding back the tears that were stinging my eyes. "I am pregnant, do you believe it? This is so messed up."

Andre tucked a lock of white hair away from my face. "I do not think it is messed up, baby." His response was quiet, considerate, and sweet enough to make butterflies burst in my stomach. "I think it is perfect."

The first tear rolled down my face. "Don't you get it, I am pregnant!" I yelled. "There's a little human growing inside of me. A person."

"And that person is our person." He took my hand and placed the sweetest kiss there. "We made that person together."

"What happens to us?" I dragged my hand away from him and mopped my cheeks. "What happens to this little person in my stomach?"

Andrei's inability to be direct was driving me insane. I knew he didn't want me, and his calculative responses showed the same. He was probably thinking of how to get rid of me right now, I could feel it in the marrow of my bones.

"Do you want that little person, *malysh?*"

I'd asked myself what Andrei wanted, but I hadn't even considered what I wanted. Bringing a child into a dirty world like ours was the last thing I wanted, and growing up with a father like mine, I wasn't sure the kind of mother I would become.

The kind who burns her child to teach it a lesson?

Or the kind who gives her child everything she wished she could have had while she was growing up?

"I don't think I'll be a good mother," I said quietly. "I'm a walking trauma, what could I possibly do for this baby?"

"Tell me, *malysh.* What are the things you wished for as a child?"

I sniffled. "A dog I'd walk to the park on weekends, bedtime stories, and cuddles whenever I was scared."

Smile lines appeared on Andrei's lips. "Those are the thing you'd do for our baby."

Chapter 26 - Andrei

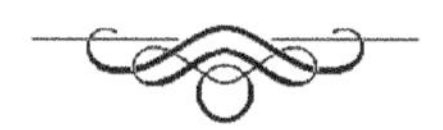

"We can't just give her back to Dante. I know she is his daughter, but he may kill her," Alexei complained. He didn't seem to like her the first time I brought her here, but he'd warmed up to her now.

"Do you think I'd hand my wife to that animal?" I put a cigarette between my lips and lit it. "I won't." I wouldn't give up either my wife or my baby.

I stared at the pool in front of us. The mere fact that I was sitting in front of the pool where that bitch Camilla almost killed Adrienne and our baby made my muscles quiver. I gritted my teeth and threw my head back on the upholstered chair to look at the sky.

The ornaments in it shone very bright, beautifully, I would reach out and pluck some stars and even the moon for Adrienne if I could. It pained me that I couldn't, being human sure came with a lot of limitations.

Alexei furrowed his brows as if he hadn't expected me to say that. "You're sensitive when it comes to her."

"And you need to get laid, maybe you'll cool off a bit."

My brother wrinkled his nose as if I'd just asked him to feast on a corpse. "Look what it's doing to you, man. I'll pass."

"No one can lay a finger on her, Alexei." Because *she's* mine, and the baby *she's* carrying was mine as well. I'd burn the whole damn world for her and my child. Damn, I liked the sound of that, *my child.*

"What are we going to do about Dante? We've held it off for too long, some of his men were caught in our warehouse yesterday."

I popped another smoke, letting it leave through my nose this time. "Adrienne will tell us all we need to know."

"She won't betray her own father," Alexei protested. "What if she's playing you?"

The chances of that were slim. She wouldn't kill the father of her baby for a father who was nothing but the gatekeeper of her hell. "I'll take my chances with her."

My phone rang, interrupting our conversation. I took it out of my pocket and checked the caller; it was Dimitri. He never called unless it was something urgent. Plus, I hadn't seen him since I returned to New York yesterday.

"*Brat!—*"

"What do you want?" I said wanting him to go straight to the point. I was so mad at him and Isidor for leaving Adrienne alone yesterday, and it was even more upsetting that they hadn't even realized what had happened while they were away.

"There is a problem," Dimitri informed me. "I'll call you once we reach the manor."

I could hear Dimitri's voice and two pairs of footsteps as they approached the pool. We hadn't told them we'd returned to New York yet. I'd wanted to give them a shock and Alexei didn't mind keeping our arrival away from them.

"Christ!" Isidor paced back as he was startled.

Dimitri joined him. He wasn't as stunned by my presence as Isidor was, but he still had his phone to his ear, a sign that I was the last person he'd expected to see.

They walked towards me and Alexei. "When did you return?"

"Really? That is what you'd ask?" I removed the almost burnt-out cigarette from my mouth, threw it on the floor, and crushed it with the sole of my shoe. "I think the appropriate thing to do is explaining where the hell you went to while Camilla tried to drown the life out of Adrienne."

Dimitri and Isidor both peered at each other before looking at me. "We didn't know she'd be around," Isidor said to their defense. He was really the most foolish one among my brothers.

"Of course you wouldn't, you fucking lunatic, "I retorted at him. "It could have been anyone for Christ's sake." I'd imagined a raid or a kidnap to get back at me since I had too many enemies and none of them would bat an eye to kidnap someone I cared about. All my brothers were well trained on how to defend themselves, even Isidor, despite his reckless behavior and slender appearance. Adrienne had some combat skills, but it was nothing in the face of real danger.

"Where is Camilla?" Dimitri asked. "How the hell did she know the perfect time to come over?"

"Maria," Alexei chimed into the conversation. "She told her."

"Fuck," Dimitri muttered. "I should have been more cautious; I didn't think shit like this would happen."

"You should have, and shit like this happens all the damn time." No matter how annoyed I was, it was really hard to stay mad at my brothers for long.

"If what we heard about Adrienne was true, then she has some fighting skills, no?" Isidor put one hand on his waist, calculating whatever it was he was calculating in his head. "How was Camilla able to fight her that easily?"

I guessed that was the part where I had to come clean. "She's pregnant."

Dimitri was the first to break the five-minute silence that filled the room. "Who, Camilla?"

I eyeballed him. "For fucks sake, no." I grimaced. "Adrienne is pregnant."

The announcement was enough to make Alexei shift in his chair.

"You knocked up Dante Paola's daughter?" Dimitri asked with his mouth wide open and his eyes trying to pop out of their sockets.

"I did, and I don't want to hear any shit about it."

"Are you keeping the baby?" I knew Isidor would be the one to disobey. I may have been too gentle on him while he was growing, and I regret it every single time I see his face.

"Yes."

"Woah!" Isidor exclaimed. "I really wasn't expecting that."

I could have said I wasn't either, but I'd fucked her raw and deep, so I wasn't exactly expecting a bag of cash in return while I did that.

"Her papa will not be excited to hear the news," Alexei said in his usual brusque tone.

"Fuck Dante, like I care what he thinks." I'd rather have him killed and buried in some faraway desert, but I couldn't do that now that Adrienne was pregnant. She may act like she didn't give two cents about him, but nevertheless, I couldn't act impulsively and hurt her.

Dimitri lit a cigarette from where he was standing. "How do you plan on handling Dante now?"

Truth is, I really hadn't come up with another solution for the fucker. Killing him had always been my intention, and I may still consider it despite knowing the effect it would have on Adrienne. He'd spilled the blood on my bed, and I needed to spill his in return. Plus, he'd been a pain in my neck since I became the leader of the Bratva, so it would be good to get him out of my way once and for all. "I'll think of something."

"And Adrienne?" Isidor's extreme concern for her was getting on my nerves. I'd have kicked him in the crotch by now if he weren't my brother.

"I'll handle Adrienne," I responded simply. "No one must speak of this again."

Clearing of throats filled the air around me, but none of them dared to ask or comment further on Adrienne being pregnant. "What is it you wanted to tell me?" My question was directed at Dimitri.

He stared at Isidor, then at me. "Isidor's fucking Barnes Chester's daughter."

Fuck. As if I hadn't dealt with enough problems for a lifetime. Barnes Chester was the new leader of the Philadelphia crime family. We weren't necessarily rivals, but we weren't allies either, so Isidor fucking a Philadelphian meant one of two things: either we formed an alliance by marriage, or we went into war. I didn't like the sound of either of them. I glared at Isidor; I could feel my ears steam at the way he was looking at the ground.

"How did you find out?" I asked Dimitri, but my eyes were glued on Isidor, whom I felt like beating the shit out of.

"Caught them fucking in a corner at the party tonight."

I twisted my wrist to look at my watch. "You have two minutes to explain yourself."

Isidor gave me his most innocent look. "I swear, I didn't fucking know who she was."

Alexei's eyes reddened with as much rage as the racing of my pulse. "You fuck bitches you don't know the identity of all the time, makes sense you'd fuck a Philly and be totally unaware."

"I'm fucking sorry, man. It was just one time."

"Well, you've gotten yourself into some deep shit. Pray that I think of a solution before Chester finds out you've been nutting in his daughter."

I stood up, went to Isidor, and gave him a hard punch in the stomach. "That's for being so fucking stupid."

He bent over and clutched his stomach with pain written all over his face. "Shit!"

He attempted to erect himself when my fist met the softness of his stomach again. "That's for the stress and negotiations you cause me."

Isidor let out a groan as he fell to his knees. I'd punch him more, but I had better things to do with my time than waste it on my idiot of a brother—better things like going to Adrienne—she was somewhere in the main building, yet it felt like she was a continent away from me. I wondered if she yearned for my presence as much as I craved hers.

The walk from the pool to my room felt like a walk through the Sahara. My feet dragged and were too slow no matter how quickly I walked. I was soon running up the stairs one leg at a time. Then I was in front of my door undressing my tie and shirt, brushing my hair to the back with my bare hands, inhaling my mouth to be certain the smell of cigarette wouldn't be enough to her make her cautious.

Adrienne was peacefully asleep when I entered my room. Truth to God, seeing her peacefully on my bed like this and knowing my baby was growing inside her sent a warmth across my chest. I didn't have alcohol, but I was getting intoxicated with something stronger than liquor.

I started brushing her hair gently; it was hard not to admit Adrienne's hair was one of the most beautiful things about her. It was as white as the first winter snow, silky, and I loved how it sheeted her shoulders. Christ, there was nothing about this woman I didn't like. *Nothing.*

She must've noticed my presence because she smiled and slowly opened her eyes. When she blinked up at me, her smile broadened. "You're here," she said, her voice cracked from sleep.

"I am, *malysh.*" I tucked into the bed beside her and she put her head on my shoulder and started drawing something invisible on my stomach.

"Camilla, you didn't kill her right?"

I may have found something I didn't like about her; it was how much she cared about people even after they hurt her, and even that was goddamn attractive.

"And Maria," she went on. "I don't want you to hurt her, she was only one of my papa's victims."

"Alright," was all I said. It was all I could reply. Because both Maria and Camilla had tried to hurt what was mine, and I didn't have it in me to show any mercy to them.

It was safe to say I'd taken them to a place they'd never return from, *ever.*

Chapter 27 - Adrienne

I knew Andrei was lying when he said he hadn't hurt Camilla, yet a part of me wished earnestly that he had at least spared Maria. It was true that she was the one who informed Camilla that Andrei was away, but that was all the part she played in what happened yesterday and I honestly didn't think it was something she deserved to die for.

It was also hard to blame Andrei if he had killed either of them. Aside from the fact that he was a ruthless Russian crime leader, I'd recognized the look in his eyes yesterday as fear. The way his dilated blue eyes bore into mine, the trembling of his hands as he held me, he must have realized he was about to lose the greatest asset he had to bring my papa down.

An asset. I guessed that was all I could ever be to him. I rubbed my hands on my belly, it was hard to shake off the feeling that right now, he only wanted me because I was carrying his child. He would probably dump me the moment I gave birth to this baby, and the idea of that made me want to hate everything about the situation I was in.

His hands caressed my cheeks, calling my attention to him as he probably realized I was distracted with thoughts. "*Malysh,* what are you thinking?"

I raised my head so that our eyes met briefly before I redirected my gaze to the tattoo on his chest. At least now I was certain Camilla was not the woman he loved, but it made me even more curious about who this woman was. My mind grew malicious as I pondered on how this woman had the heart that would never be mine. "This woman," I started, trailing the lines of the skull on his tattoo. "Do you still miss her?"

"Yes," Andrei said in an undertone. "I miss her even more now that I have reminders of her all over."

My chest felt like it was being tied together by the string as tears penetrated them. I didn't like being lied to, but I would have preferred a lie to the heart-shattering truth he gave me. I tried to remove my hand from Andrei's chest, but he caught it and placed his hand over it. I could feel the beating of his heart, fast, strong, and for another woman.

"Does it hurt you that I miss another woman?"

It does, and I don't even know why, was what I wanted say, but I turned my face away from him and lied instead. "No, you and I, we are nothing more than enemies who fucked."

"And enemies who're gonna have a baby together," he helped me complete. "Jesus, Adrienne, is that all you think of what we are doing?"

"Is there anything more?" I turned to look at him. "Do you have something more to offer me?" His heart was the only thing I wanted, but it was already taken by another woman. What more could he have to offer when he had already denied me what I really wanted?

"Everything." His hands moved from my hair and rested on my stomach. "You have everything that is mine, *malysh.*"

By everything, was he referring to the child I was carrying? A child we hadn't even met yet?

"You have a part of me in you that no one has ever had," he said firmly. "And everything that is mine is yours now, *malysh.*"

I took my hand to his left chest. "Including this?"

His eyes sparkled beautifully like a blue diamond placed under the sun. "Is it my life you want?" He stretched his hand to the nightstand, brought out a blade, and fixed it in my hands. "Know this now, you are the only one who has the right to take my life. Only you." He moved my hands so that the blade was pointing at the part of his chest where his heart was.

I closed my eyes, imagining what would happen if I drove the blade straight into his heart. If I managed to leave his manor before his brothers found out he was dead. I'd go back to my papa and prove to him that I was just as good as the son he always wanted.

And the baby, I could raise it alone and it would never find out its papa died by my own hands. But that was far from what I truly wanted. I'd sworn to kill Andrei Levov, but now I couldn't think of having anyone other than him by my side. I could not imagine kissing and fucking anyone that wasn't him.

"It is not your life I want," I spat out bitterly, letting the blade fall from my hand. "I want your heart and I know it's something I can never have."

A half smile formed on Andrei's lips, he tossed the blade to the floor and pulled me over to sit on top of him. "And what would you do with my heart if you had it?"

"Possibly toss it on the ground"—love it—"stomp on it"—and cherish it—"and throw into the trash."

"You're crazy, *malysh,*" Andrei said, amusement dancing in his eyes. "And I like you even more because of that."

"But you don't love me."

He froze.

I forgot how to breathe.

We stared at each other.

"God, baby." He gripped my waist, making my clitoris brush on his hard dick. Only a psycho like him could have an erection during a conversation like this, and I was just as much of a psycho as he was because I needed to be satisfied—pulled onto him and ride him till I came. "You think I don't love you?"

"I know you don't."

"That's bullshit, baby." I loved the way he called me *baby;* I think I loved it as much as I loved when he called me *malysh.* "I would burn the whole fucking world to the ground if you ask it of me, I would lay my life at your feet if need be for it, I want to worship the very ground you walk on. If that isn't love, then I don't know what the hell it is."

"Wait...did you just—"

"I'll kill every single person who touches you, *malysh.*" He held his hand over my belly. "Fuck, you don't know how much I want to give the world to you and our baby."

A tear rolled down my eyes without warning. I glanced away in shame, *these fucking pregnancy hormones.* "How about her?" I asked, because no matter what he said to me and how much he tried to prove his feelings, I knew I'd always be a shadow of the woman he didn't even think me important enough to tell about. "Will you always love her?"

"That woman was your mama."

My jaw slackened as soon as the words hit me. "What?" I slapped my hand over my mouth, my heart thudding."

"And I was not in love with her," he added, lifting half the weight of the shock away from my shoulder. "Your mama and I had been friends for years." A sad smile formed on his lips. "She looked just like you, white hair, grey eyes, and a sass that spiced her beauty."

Andrei paused for a minute. "She drew this tattoo on me when I became the leader of the Bratva, and sadly, that was the same day your grandfather gave her away to Dante Paolo and I fucking regret that I didn't stop her leaving."

I breathed, deeply, like I'd been submerged in water for hours and only just been pulled out. "What happened?"

"I never heard from her again until one day I found out she was dead for a few years." There was a fire in Andrei's eyes, anger that could burn through thick flesh. "I didn't even know she had a baby."

"And my name on your chest?"

"After we met the first time and I found out you were Dante's daughter, I knew you were Isabella's too." *My mama's name is Isabella.* "I got a tattoo to remember your name because that is what she would have wanted."

My heart stuttered, crumbling against my chest. I hadn't met my mama before, but this explains everything. The picture on his wall, the face staring back at me in my dreams…and the screams…the fucking screams. "Do you know how my mama died?"

Andrei shook his head. "No. I didn't even know she'd died until years later. I'd heard she died giving birth and the child she bore was a stillbirth, but I started to doubt that after I met you."

I dreaded the possibility of the next question I was about to ask. "Do you think my papa killed her?"

"I don't think Dante would do something as stupid as that."

Knowing my papa, I was certain his doing something stupid out of anger was something to be considered, I'd lived with him long enough to know how much of a beast he became when things didn't go his way. I shook my head. "No, you can't trust him not to hurt her. You said he'd been your rival since forever, what if he was jealous or something?"

My breaths were shallow and irregular as anger and sadness collided with each other, raising a storm inside me. "Why would he lie about her death and my existence if he didn't do something foolish?" I grabbed Andrei's hand with a desperate plea. "You must help me bring my papa down, please."

Andrei nodded.

"One more thing," I breathed. "You said you'd burn the world to the ground for me."

I waited for him to respond. He nodded again.

"You don't have to do that." Because there was something more that I wanted him to do, something harder than simply burning the world to the ground. "Save the world with me instead."

He narrowed his eyes to hint he had no idea what I meant. I tried to calm myself because I knew my request could be met with utter rejection.

"What would you do if we had a daughter?"

A glee reflected on Andrei's countenance. "Are you asking, *malysh?*" He ran a finger on my lips. "I'd protect her with my own life."

I gave him an inclining nod. "Of course you will." *Help me God.* "Have you ever thought of those women you have trafficked? The women who are kidnapped, drugged, and raped under your watch?"

Andrei's eyes upturned. It was possible my words were getting through to him, but I had to keep my expectations low.

"They're daughters, loved by other people the same way you'll love ours." I collected his hand from my face and placed kisses there. "Don't you think it's time to put an end to it?"

He clenched his jaw, and his eyes darkened. He was every bit the bloody mafia boss I heard him to be, not my Andrei or the father of my child, just Andrei the bloodsucker.

I expected him to push me away from his body, curse at me or even punish me the way my papa used to, but his gaze brightened, and his throat moved as he swallowed. "I will, *malysh,*" he said to my surprise. "No more using women."

Relief overtook the nerves that had worked up in my anticipation of what Andrei's response would be. I smiled because it was clearer than day, that this man here, this man whom I hated with my being, would do anything for me.

Because he was my person.

CHAPTER 28 - ADRIENNE

I sniffled the smell of omelets and fried beef. I hadn't eaten those in so long and I don't know if it was because of the baby, but now that I perceived them, I had a feeling I'd crave them all day.

I'd fallen asleep on Andrei's chest while discussing possible unisex baby names for the little Levov growing inside of me. Andrei had chosen Liliya because he was positive it would be a little girl that we'd cherish like the lily flower. I'd had a different opinion though; I'd chosen Aleksis because I had a strong feeling it would be a boy.

We'd gone ahead and made a bet on one of us granting the winner a wish. I giggled because I knew I'd be right. I had to start thinking of what wish I'd ask Andrei to fulfill. I moved my hands behind me in search of Andrei. I supposed he'd rolled away from me in his sleep but quickly opened my eyes when I realized the bed was empty.

Sunlight poured into the room, lighting dust particles in the air. I glanced around, noticing the portrait of my mother on the wall had disappeared, I figured I could find where it went later, for now, I had to find a way to satisfy my omelet cravings, but not before finding out who dared to soil the air with such a sweet aroma.

We haven't had a cook since Maria left two days ago, so it made me wonder if Andrei had gotten a new cook already. I ambled to the bathroom to use the toilet and take a quick shower before going down to the kitchen.

"Good morning, *malysh,*" met me as soon as I walked inside the kitchen. We didn't have a new cook, but I'd genuinely take the sight in front of me over a new cook, truly. Andrei was standing in front of the counter, stirring something with one hand while giving me a smile that caused my breath to cease for a good minute.

He was wearing a pair of baggy shorts with nothing to cover his toned abs and muscular chest except the ink on his chest and arms. My eyes trailed every single detail on his body, and my heartbeat accelerated. I bit my lower lip because the only thing I could think of was the weight of his body on mine as he fucked me. *God!*

I walked over to him, taking in the scent of omelets and the sexy chef in the kitchen. "You know how to cook?"

"Yeah, being the oldest of four kids makes you learn that quite easily," he said, his focus on the beef he was stirring.

"Wow!" Who would have thought a day would come when Andrei-fucking-Levov would be making me breakfast in his kitchen? The end of the world must've been truly near. "I'd never thought a ruthless mafia boss would have any skills other than killing."

He shark-smiled, his eyes glowing like the sky when the sun was scorching. "I don't have many skills, other than leading a group of nasty men, making the best breakfast—" he reduced the fire from the stove, and turned to me, mischief written all over his face. "—and fucking you."

My cheeks ignited, spreading a fire that needed to be quenched to my clitoris. This man was something, truth to God. "Are you bragging, Mr. Levov?"

Andrei pressed his body against mine then held my two legs and lifted me onto the cabinet. "I am. Do you have a problem with that, Mrs. Levov?"

It was hard not to smile when this man was poking my heart with such cheesiness. "Mrs. Levov?"

He kissed my forehead. "Yes, Mrs. Levov." His kiss moved to my neck. "Did you think I'd taint your name by letting you remain unmarried while you're carrying my child?"

The air was hot around me, as if I was burning in the hell of my own desire. "Are you asking me to marry you, Mr. Levov?"

"I'm not asking, baby." His hand slid in between my thighs. "I'm telling you; you do not get to turn me down."

An unexpected moan left my throat as his hand brushed lightly with my clitoris. "Well, I do not see a ring, Mr. future-husband."

"A ring can wait." His hand trailed its way under my gown and he groped one of my breasts while a finger from his other hand sought entrance into my pussy. "An orgasm is what you need now."

Yep, only Andrei could be making a proposal with an orgasm. "How about my papa?"

"I'll deal with him before we get married."

I pushed him back. "What about your brothers? They may come inside while you're in your orgasm-giving-mission."

He smiled dangerously. "I locked them out."

"What?" I burst into a hearty laugh. "Are you serious?"

He nodded.

"Why the fuck would you do that?" I asked, trying to control my laughter.

"I needed time alone with you, and I also figured it'd be best if they got their own fucking places." His eyes were on me, but his fingers were working their way between my thighs.

"Will you be okay living without them?"

"All I need is you, *malysh*." His sultry voice penetrated me like a sharp-edged sword. "All I need is you. I want to take you to my clubs and show you off to the whole world."

Andrei was strange today, and I liked how strange he was. "Today, after you've had enough rest."

"Won't your underlings be furious? I'm their enemy's daughter."

"And you'll be their queen from tonight on." His fingers slid into my pussy and my throat evoked a moan. He parted my thighs and lowered himself between my legs. "Will you marry me, *malysh?*"

"No," I replied, mainly to provoke him into fucking my brains out.

"Brace yourself, baby. You may come to regret that answer."

I gave him a teasing smile. "Make me."

His wet tongue started out by kissing the warm moist fold of my thighs, sending signals all over my body. I took his hand to my nipples, encouraging him to squeeze them hard the way he did the first time he fucked me.

He took his time moving his tongue from my thighs to my clitoris and gave it a light lick before taking his mouth up to one of my nipples, sucking it hard while moving his finger inside of me.

My whole body vibrated to his touch, the way his hands knew the spot to hit, the way his tongue knew how to drive me out of my senses. I gripped the counter to stop myself from moaning loudly but it was futile, completely. Every part of me was mixed with fire and ice, all nerves in my body were in action.

Andrei pulled his finger from my pussy and forced it into my lips. "Taste yourself, baby," he commanded. "Do you like it?"

I devoured every flavor of mine on his finger, groaning my response to him. "Yeah, I fucking like it."

"Good girl," he whispered into my ear, sending a rush of pleasure up my spine.

He pushed me back on the counter and pulled my thighs out so he could get a further view of me. "I'm going to eat you till you give me the answer I need." He slid two fingers inside me again while caressing my clitoris with his tongue. It was a good thing we didn't have neighbors because I was certain they'd be concerned with how loud I was moaning.

I started riding his finger, craving for him inside me. "Please, Andrei," I gasped. "I want you to fuck me now, please."

"*Nyet, malysh.*" He started sliding his finger in and out of me. "Not until you give me the answer I want."

The counter wasn't doing a good enough job at keeping me from screaming my pleasure out. I gripped Andrei's hair, strong enough to make him bald by the time we were done.

He didn't seem to mind because he increased the speed of his tongue on my clitoris. "Will you marry me, Adrienne?" The question came through his own moan, it was so fucking sexy, and my body was responding to it in a nice way. My insides tensed, my pulse tripled. "I will marry you."

"Scream it, baby. I want the whole world to hear your answer."

His tongue pressed harder to my clitoris and I felt like I was a ticking bomb waiting to explode. "I'll marry you Andrei Levov, I'll fucking marry—oh my God, oh my God." Orgasm took over my words, and I fucking exploded. My legs were jerking without control, my grip on the counter and Andrei's hair tightened, and I filled the kitchen with my screams. Only Andrei could make me feel this way, only him.

"Come for me, baby," Andrei demanded, rubbing his wet thumb all over my clitoris.

My body was still broken from the orgasm when he dragged me down from the counter and spun me around so that my breasts and head were resting on the soft white wood. My body tingled as I felt Andrei's dick, warm and erect, behind me. I wanted him, I wanted all of him.

He slid into me, gentle and soft, not like the first or second time we fucked. I felt like he was being careful not to hurt me or the baby, and I didn't want him to be careful, I wanted him to fuck me with as much carelessness as he did before.

I tried to turn around but a spank on my ass kept me in place—my cheeks must've felt the spank more because they flushed with hotness. "Fuck me, Andrei, I want you to fuck me hard."

"Baby, I don't—"

"Forget about hurting me and the baby, I want you to fuck me like I'm your dirty little slut."

Andrei cupped one of my breasts from behind. "I'll fuck you like you're my whore, because you're mine, understand?" He thrust inside me.

I nodded.

"I want to hear you say it."

"I'm yours," I said, my voice laced with an after-effect of my orgasm.

His thrusts were slow at first, but with each minute they increased until we both climaxed.

We climbed up to the room to wash off the essence of sex from ourselves. The food had gone cold before we returned.

CHAPTER 29 - ANDREI

I didn't take Adrienne to the other clubs she'd been to; I chose to take her to the biggest Levov club in New York. The one where the richest guys with the biggest influence in the city came to have fun at night. I'd wanted to show her off to the whole fucking world and mark her as mine. I also wanted to make it clear that no one was allowed to touch her or hurt her.

Flickering that bore my eyes to death welcomed us into the club as we entered, where strippers on heels and spoiled rich kids danced the night away, the smell of alcohol and cigarettes clouding the atmosphere. I watched Adrienne to make sure she wasn't irritated by the smell or sound, but she seemed okay with it.

"This is the biggest club you own?" Her loud voice pierced the air.

I nodded.

"It's really nice," she said with a gleam touching her face. Her eyes sparkled in the lights, and the smell of her perfume seeped into my senses. "Can we dance?"

I wasn't pleased with that question. I looked at her from head to toe, the hairs on my neck standing up at the thought of other men seeing her dance in that red short dress that clung to every curve on her body. "No."

She pouted, making my eyes soften without her even insisting. "Just one dance," I said in defeat. "I'll sit and watch."

She gave me her broadest smile and kissed my cheeks. "You're a darling."

I hadn't recovered before she pushed me onto one of the cushions at the edge of the wall. She winked at me and my damn cock nodded in response. I lit a cigarette because I may fucking have to bulge out every single male eye that looked at what was mine.

Adrienne started to dance, moving like a fucking python seducing its prey, swaying her hips from side to side. Now I wanted to grab her and fuck her again. I kept my eyes on every guy around her, glaring at whoever dared to look at her for more than a second.

One of the guys was dumb and he decided to defile me as he walked to Adrienne. She moved and her back hit his chest. She smiled at him, and I gritted my teeth even though I knew she was just apologizing for hitting him. She turned away and the fucker leaned over and said something into her ear, making her spin to him with a wrinkled face.

After a few exchanges of words, she turned away from him and continued dancing. Then he did the most stupid thing by grabbing her wrist. My adrenaline pumped faster than the speed of light as I rushed out of my seat. Adrienne had kicked him in the balls before I reached where they were. The fucker raised his hand to hit her, but I caught it mid-air.

"You have a problem with my wife?" I growled.

His stupidity must've stared him back in his fucking face because terror overtook the boldness he had when he was harassing my woman. "Wife?" He glanced at Adrienne and then at me. "I'm sorry, I swear I didn't know she was yours."

"Now you know." A wicked smile crossed my face. "And you'll pay for your recklessness."

Adrienne held my arm. "Just let him go, I'm sure he didn't mean to."

I shot her a glare to silence her. I didn't appreciate how she made excuses for jackasses all the time.

"Kneel and beg," I said to the guy.

He got on his knees without hesitation. It amused me how idiots like him had no issue harassing women but would easily crumble to their knees in front of men like me. "I'm sorry," he stuttered. "I didn't know you were his, I swear."

Adrienne peered around the club. Nearly all eyes were on us. she didn't accept or decline his apology, but I thought to give him something he'd remember me for.

I removed the blade I always carried around from my pocket. "Choose a finger."

He started trembling, tears filling his eyes. "No, please—"

"I'll take it that you want me to make a choice for you." I took the index finger on the hand he'd used to touch my woman, pressed my blade to it, and watched as it slowly parted his knuckles. His screams were silenced by the loud music, his blood poured like smoke from an old engine. I didn't stop till half of his finger was on the floor.

I leaned close to his ear, satisfied with my cruelty. "Don't ever touch a woman who doesn't want to be touched by you." He was still yelling from pain when I wiped his disgusting blood on his black shirt to clean my blade before sliding it back into my jacket.

I was met with Adrienne's unflinching look when I turned at her. She had her hands crossed angrily over her chest and she glared at me as if she wanted to reach out to break my neck.

"What now?" I asked, sensing the anger that was steaming from her stare.

She hissed and walked away, making me chase after her while yelling her name like I was a fucking lunatic. "Why the hell are you mad at me?" I grabbed her by the arm when we reached the red hallway leading to my office and swiveled her so she could look at me.

"Are you serious?" she bellowed. "You just chopped off a man's finger and you're asking why the hell I'm mad at you?"

"He touched you."

"That isn't enough reason to chop off his damned fingers," she retorted with a deafening roar. "For God's sake Andrei, must you react violently to send a message across?

"What do you want me to do?" I placed my hand on the wall above her. "Seeing another man breathe the same air you do infuriates me, let alone watching one touch you."

Something twinkled in her eyes, as if her anger was melting away. "God, Andrei." She raised her hand, touching my cheeks very delicately. "I don't think I can bear to see another woman touch you, I'd be damned before I let that happen, but I can't kill or hurt everyone that tries to because I trust you enough to know you wouldn't do something that'd hurt me."

I kissed her and slid a hand around her waist. "I won't do that anymore if it bothers you." That was a lie, I'd do it over and over again, just not in her presence.

"Fine," she nodded.

"Fine," I repeated after her. My cock was reacting to her presence. I leaned in for a kiss before I heard the most annoying voice ever.

"Brother."

I hit the wall in frustration before looking over to the source of the annoying voice. Dimitri and Isidor were standing in front of the mahogany door leading into my office. "What the fuck do you want."

"There's a problem," Alexei's voice chimed in as he joined us. "Dante Paolo knows where his daughter is." His eyes were on Adrienne. I could sense his dislike for her, but I knew he wouldn't hurt her, because she was mine.

"You didn't think to tell me earlier?"

"I'd have told you if only you picked up your damn cell."

I put my hand into my pocket and removed my phone. I had ten missed calls from Alexei and six more from Dimitri.

"My papa won't sit back if he knows I'm here, he'd put—" Adrienne was still talking when a gunshot came from the club. I dragged her down to cover her.

"Fuck." I took out my .45 from my pocket and cocked it, then looked over at Dimitri. "If anything happens to her, you're dead." Then I signaled Alexei and Isidor to come with me.

"You can't leave me here," Adrienne protested. "I'm coming."

"No, you're not."

"Yes, I am."

"This is not the time to be so damn stubborn, *malysh*." I had to take care of her stubbornness after I'd dealt with Dante. "Stay here and keep our baby safe." I didn't wait for her retort before I left her.

Dante was sitting on one of my cushions, smoking with a shot of my branded liquor in his hand. Some of my men lay dead on the floor, along with some of his, while the ones alive had their guns pointed at each other.

"What the fuck are you doing here?" I growled with my gun pointed at his head.

"You have something that's mine, I've come to collect it." His voice was calm yet filled with venom. He blew smoke from his nose.

"Nothing here belongs to you, Dante. Now get the fuck out of my club."

He laughed hoarsely in a way that irritated my ears. "I'm not leaving without her."

"Adrienne is not a property, and she is the only reason I haven't put a bullet in your head yet." My anger was increasing with every minute and I wasn't sure how long I'd be able to play the good mafia boss before I pulled the trigger on this asshole.

"Come on, Andrei." He sipped *my* liquor. "We both know women are nothing but commodities in my world."

"Looks like our world needs to evolve then."

"Women are commodities, just like my mama was?" Adrienne came out from the hallway, pointing a gun at Dante with Dimitri behind her. Dimitri's eyes met mine apologetically and I understood it wasn't his fault. Adrienne gets what Adrienne wants.

Dante's eyes flickered with shock. "You know nothing about your mama."

"I do know that you killed her," Adrienne said, returning the chilly calmness in Dante's voice; she was playing his game with him.

"I didn't."

Bang. One of Dante's men fell to the ground as smoke spilled from the gun Adrienne was holding. His other men pointed their guns at her, but Dante raised a hand, signaling them not to shoot. "Tell another lie, Papa, and I'll drill another bullet in the head of all your men until there are none left."

I couldn't have been prouder of my girl than I was in that moment. I loved badass Adrienne.

"Your mama was sick after she gave birth to you," Dante explained. "I didn't fucking kill her."

Bang. Another Italian man fell to the floor, dead.

"I heard her scream before she died," Adrienne growled.

Dante sighed furiously. "She had a damn heart attack; I didn't kill her."

Adrienne's eyes glittered with tears, but she did a good job of keeping them from falling. "I won't return with you; I am getting married to Andrei."

"You're crazy, I won't let you marry that bastard."

"I am not asking for your permission." She cocked her gun, pointing it directly at Dante's heart. "I'm having his baby."

"You're just a *puttana* like your mother was," Dante cursed. Only a lunatic like him would call his daughter a whore.

Adrienne unloaded two bullets on another two Italians, bringing the number of Dante's men to three against the twelve I had inside the club. It would be a piece of cake to kill him now if I wanted to. "I am," Adrienne inclined. "But I am also a killer because you made me one."

Her hands were shaking and tears were rolling down her cheeks. "From now on, I'm a Levov, not your daughter. If one girl goes missing from this city after tonight, I won't give a fuck if it's your doing or not, I'll put a bullet in your head. If any girl is raped by an Italian, I'll burn your dirty money to the ground and make sure you have nothing left. Do you understand me?"

Dante did not respond.

Adrienne targeted her bullet at the shot he was holding, shattering it and leaving a narrow cut on Dante's hand. "Do you fucking understand me?"

Dante gave a reluctant nod.

"Now get the fuck out of my fiancée's club."

Dante and the three men he still had standing took a walk of shame out of the club. Adrienne's tears were falling harder now, and her hands were quivering as she kept her gun pointed in the direction her papa had just left from.

I went to her, took the gun, and cleaned her tears. "You did well, *malysh*." I tilted her head up and gazed into her twinkling gray eyes. "You did well."

"Fuck," she sniffled. "I thought I'd become weak when I saw him and mess it all up." She gave me a beautiful smile through her tears.

"But you didn't, because you're a Levov, *malysh*."

"I am a Levov," she confirmed. "Come with me." She dragged me to the hall where we'd argued before Dante interrupted our peace, picked her purse from the floor, and brought out a pair of cufflinks. "I got these for you, I didn't know if you'd like them since I bought them with your money."

I took the diamonds from her. "No one has ever gotten me a gift, not even my brothers." She was beaming with pride, and happiness, her lashes still wet with tears. "I didn't know I'd ever say these words to anyone, but God, I fucking love you, Adrienne."

Her cheeks turned red under the warm white light in the hall. "I love you too, Andrei. With my whole heart."

I slowly leaned down to her, parted her mouth, and kissed her softly on the lips. I didn't give a fuck if I had five minutes to live or if this woman would someday drive a knife into my heart. I just wanted to love her.

Till the day I took my last breath.

EPILOGUE - ADRIENNE

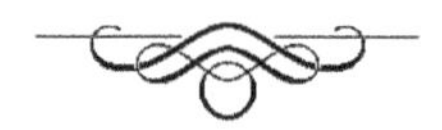

Eight months later…

"It's a girl!" Andrei announced to the room at large, filled with glee and a kind of excitement I'd never seen him wear. "It's a baby girl."

The doctor and nurse gave me a knowing smile before giving us our privacy.

Andrei came to me and placed the baby in my arms. "She looks just like me," he boasted. It wasn't a lie; she had his dark hair and the same blue eyes the Levovs were known for. "Looks like you lost the bet, Mrs. Levov."

I gave a weak smile; twenty hours of labor was no joke for this cute tiny human to come out looking just like her papa. "What do you want, husband?"

He seemed lost in thought for a second, before whispering his answer into my ear. "Kiss me."

"A kiss?"

He nodded.

"That is all you want with a wish like that?" I rolled my eyes at how naughty he was, suddenly feeling strong enough to give a wide grin. "Choose wisely, Mr. Levov, you may never get an opportunity like this one again."

"That is what I want," he insisted.

"Alright." I wrapped one of my hands around his neck and pulled him down then pressed my lips on his cheeks when the door flew open.

Three giant Levovs entered inside with balloons, confetti, and teddy bears in both blue and pink.

"I can't believe I'm now an uncle." Isidor took the baby from my arms. "Is it a boy?"

Dimitri smacked him on the head. "That's obviously a girl, you imbecile."

"Does she have a name yet?" Alexei asked, taking the baby from Isidor. He was smiling so brightly that it warmed my heart.

"Liliya," I said. "It was the name Andrei had chosen, and seeing how beautiful she is, it felt right to give her that name."

"Liliya Aleksis Levov," Andrei completed, rubbing Liliya's head gently.

"Welcome to the world, Liliya," Alexei said with a smile.

With one look at the Levov boys, I knew Liliya would have the best men in the world around her. Andrei would be a good father, and his brothers would be the best uncles to my daughter. There was nothing more I could ask for when I was already blessed with a family like this one.

And I could not request a love greater than the one Andrei and I shared.

THE END

About Deva Blake

Deva Blake writes from her study room with garden view in her Californian home. She loves having a cup of mint tea as well as a rose candle burning next to her while working. Deva writes dark mafia romance about the type of guys that your parents warned you about but that you end up falling for anyway, because they're just too irresistible. When not buried in her dark imagination, she enjoys baking cakes for her son and husband.

BOOKS BY DEVA BLAKE

"Levov Bratva" Series

The Bratva of New York are the most ruthless, merciless and possessive mobsters of the city. They take what they want, break what they please, and heal what they deem worthy. But will they take the biggest risk of all: open their heart for the one they've claimed?

The Bratva's Kidnapped Bride

The Bratva's Secret Baby

Printed in Great Britain
by Amazon